American Tall Tales

American ☆

ADRIEN STOUTENBURG

✶ ✶ all Tales

Illustrated by Richard M. Powers

Puffin Books

Penguin Books Ltd, Harmondsworth, Middlesex, England
Penguin Books, 40 West 23rd Street, New York, New York 10010, U.S.A.
Penguin Books Australia Ltd, Ringwood, Victoria, Australia
Penguin Books Canada Limited, 2801 John Street, Markham, Ontario, Canada L3R 1B4
Penguin Books (N.Z.) Ltd, 182-190 Wairau Road, Auckland 10, New Zealand

First published by The Viking Press 1966
Viking Seafarer Edition published 1969
Reprinted 1972
Published in Puffin Books 1976
Reprinted 1982, 1984, 1985, 1986

Library of Congress Cataloging in Publication Data
Stoutenburg, Adrien   American tall tales.
Summary: Features eight American folk heroes: Paul
Bunyan, Pecos Bill, Stormalong, Mike Fink, Davy Crockett,
Johnny Appleseed, John Henry, and Joe Magarac.
1. Tales, American. [1. Folklore–United States]
I. Powers, Richard M. II. Title.
[PZ8.1.S887Am6] 398.2′2′0973 76–28350
ISBN 0–14–030928–4

Printed in the United States of America by
Offset Paperback Mfrs., Inc., Dallas, Pennsylvania

To that special friend
James R. K. Kantor

Contents

American Tall Tales

Sky-bright Axe

Some people say that Paul Bunyan wasn't much taller than an ordinary house. Others say he must have been a lot taller to do all the things he did, like sticking trees into his pockets and blowing birds out of the air when he sneezed. Even when he was a baby, up in Maine, he was so big he knocked down a mile of trees just by rolling over in his sleep.

Everyone was nervous about what might happen when Baby Paul grew older and started crawling. Maine wouldn't have any forests left.

Paul's father, who was an ordinary-sized man, was a bit nervous about it all himself. One night he had wakened to find his bed down on the floor. There beside it sat Baby Paul, a crosscut saw in one hand. In the other hand he held one of the sawed-off legs of the bed. He was chewing on it to help his teeth grow.

"I'll have to put him somewhere safe," Paul's father decided, "where he won't be a public nuisance."

He cut down some tall trees growing near his own cabin and built a boat shaped like a cradle. Paul's mother tucked Paul into it. Then Paul's parents put a long rope on the floating cradle and let it drift out to sea a little way.

It was a lovely, blue-green place for a cradle, with fish flashing around and the waves making small, humpbacked motions underneath. Baby Paul sucked his thumb and watched the seagulls flying over, light shaking from beneath their wings. Paul smiled, and then he hiccoughed. The hiccough started a gale that nearly blew a fishing boat all the way to the North Pole.

Finally, Paul went to sleep. He snored so loudly the gulls went flapping toward land for they thought a thunderstorm was coming. Then young Paul had a bad dream, brought on by the extra-large ham his mother had given him for breakfast. He tossed about in his sleep and started the cradle rocking. Each time the cradle rocked it sent a wave as big as a building toward shore. Paul tossed harder, and the waves grew even larger, bigger than cities. They smashed against the shore and threatened to drown everything on land.

People scampered up church steeples. They scrambled onto roof tops. They clawed their way up into trees, and they yelled for the government to save them. The settlers for miles around put rifles on their shoulders and marched up to Paul's father.

"Get that baby out of here!" they shouted. "He's a danger to the whole state. A baby like that is against the Constitution!"

Paul's father, and his mother, too, couldn't help feeling a bit proud of how strong Paul was. But they knew that the smartest thing to do was to move away. No one seems to know exactly where they went. Wherever it was, Paul didn't cause too much trouble for the rest of the time he was growing up. His father taught him certain things which helped.

"Don't lean too hard against smallish trees or buildings, Son," his father told him. "And if there are towns or farmers' fields in your way, step around them."

And Paul's mother told him, "Never pick on anybody who isn't your own size, Son."

Since there wasn't anyone his size around, Paul never got into fights. Being taller than other boys, by about fifty feet or so, he was naturally the best hunter, fisherman, walker, runner, yeller, or mountain climber there was. And he was best of all at cutting down trees and turning them into lumber. In those days, when America was new, people had to cut down a lot of trees. They needed the lumber for houses, churches, town halls, ships, bridges, ballrooms, stores, pencils, wagons, and flag poles. Luckily, the trees were there, stretching in tall, wind-shining rows across America. The trees marched up mountains and down again. They followed rivers and creeks. They massed up together in purple canyons and shoved each other out of the way on the shores of lakes. They pushed their dark roots down into rock and their glossy branches into the clouds.

Paul liked to flash a sky-bright axe over his head. He loved the smell of wood when it was cut and the look of its sap gleaming like honey. He didn't chop trees down in any ordinary way. With four strokes he would lop all the limbs and bark off a tree, making it a tall, square post. After he had squared up miles of forest in a half-hour, he would take an axe head and tie a long rope to it. Then he would stand straddle-legged and swing the axe in a wide circle, yelling, "T-I-M-B-E-R-R-R! Look out!" With every swing and every yell, a hundred trees would come whooshing down.

The fallen trees had to be hauled down to a river so that they could be floated to a sawmill. Paul grew a bit tired of lugging bundles of trees under his arms, and he wished he had a strong friend to help him. Also, at times he felt lonely, not having anyone his size around.

About the time he was feeling loneliest, there came the Winter of the Blue Snow. Paul, who was full-grown by then, had never seen anything like the blue flakes falling from the sky. Nobody else had either, and perhaps they never will, unless it happens again. The blue snow fell softly at first, like bits of sky drifting down. The wind rose and the flakes grew thicker. The blue snow kept falling, day after day. It covered branches and roof tops, hill and valley, with blue, and Paul thought it was about as beautiful a sight as anyone could want.

One day when Paul was out walking in the blue snow, he stumbled over something the size of a mountain. The mountain made a faint mooing sound and shuddered.

"Excuse me," said Paul and looked closer.

Two huge, hairy ears stuck up above the snowdrift. The ears were as blue as the snow.

"Who are you?" Paul asked. There was no answer. Paul grabbed both of the ears and pulled.

Out of the snow came a shivering, clumsy, completely blue baby ox. Even its round, blinking eyes and its tail were blue. Only its shiny nose was black. The calf was the largest Paul had ever seen. Strong as he was, he felt his muscles shake under the creature's weight.

"Ah! Beautiful blue baby!" Paul said. He cradled the half-frozen calf in his great arms and carried it home. There he wrapped the baby ox in warm blankets and sat up all night taking care of it. The calf did not show much sign of life until morning. Then, as the dawn light came through the window, the ox calf stood up. The calf stretched its neck out and sloshed its wet tongue lovingly against Paul's neck.

Paul gave a roar of laughter, for his one ticklish spot was his neck.

Paul patted the baby ox and scratched his silky, blue ears. "We will be wonderful friends, eh Babe? You will be a giant of an ox and carry forests for me on your back."

That is how it happened that Babe the Blue Ox went with Paul Bunyan when Paul started out into the world to do his mighty logging work. By that time, Babe had his full growth. People never could figure out how long Babe was. They had to use field glasses even to see from one end of Babe to the other. And there were no scales large enough to weigh Babe. Paul did measure the distance between Babe's eyes, and that was exactly forty-two axe handle lengths and one plug of tobacco. Every time Babe needed new iron shoes for his hoofs, a fresh iron mine had to be opened. The shoes were so heavy that a man couldn't carry one without sinking up to his knees in solid rock.

Paul and the Blue Ox logged all over the northern timber country, from Maine to Michigan, Wisconsin, and Minnesota. Paul hired many men to help him. These lumberjacks liked working for Paul Bunyan, because he was always good to them and made sure that they had plenty of food.

The lumber crews liked pancakes best, but they would gobble

up and slurp down the pancakes so fast that the camp cooks couldn't keep up with them, even when the cooks got up twenty-six hours before daylight. The main problem was that the griddles the cooks used for frying the pancakes were too small.

The winter that Paul was logging on the Big Onion River in Michigan, he decided that he had to do something about making a big enough griddle. He went down to the plow works at Moline, Illinois, and said, "I want you fellows here to make me a griddle so big I won't be able to see across it on a foggy day."

The men set to work. When they were finished, they had built a griddle so huge there was no train or wagon large enough to carry it.

"Let me think what to do," said Paul. "We'll have to turn the griddle up on end, like a silver dollar, and roll it up to Michigan." He hitched the Blue Ox to the upturned griddle, and away they went. It wasn't any job at all for Babe and Paul, though they had to hike a couple of hundred miles. A few miles from the Big Onion lumber camp, Paul unhitched Babe and let the griddle roll on by itself. When it stopped rolling, it started to spin as a penny does when it's ready to fall. It spun around and around and dug a deep hole in the ground before it flopped down like a cover over the hole.

The lumberjacks cheered and rushed off to haul a few acres of trees into the hole for a fire. The cook and a hundred and one helpers mixed tons of batter. When everything was ready, with the flames under the griddle blazing like a forest fire, Paul picked out a crew of men who could stand the heat better than others. He had them strap fat, juicy slabs of bacon on their feet.

"You men skate around on that griddle and that'll keep it well greased," he told them.

The men skated until the griddle shone with bacon fat. White batter came pouring out onto the griddle and soon the smell of crisp, brown, steaming pancakes was drifting across the whole state. There were tons of pancakes—with plenty left over for Babe, who could eat a carload in one gulp.

There wasn't much Paul couldn't do, especially with Babe's help. But there was one job that seemed almost too hard even for him. That was in Wisconsin, on the St. Croix River. The logging road there was so crooked, it couldn't find its own way through the timber. It would start out in one direction, then turn around and go every which way until it grew so snarled up it didn't know its beginning from its end. The teamsters hauling logs over it would start home for camp and meet themselves coming back.

Maybe even Babe couldn't pull the kinks and curves out of a road as crooked as that one, Paul thought, but there was nothing to do but try.

He gave Babe several extra pats as he put the Blue Ox's pulling harness on. Then he hitched Babe to the end of the road and stood back.

Babe lowered his head and pushed his hoofs into the earth. His muscles stood out like rows of blue hills. He strained forward, pulling at the road. He stretched so hard that his hind legs spraddled out until his belly nearly scraped the ground. The road just lay there, stubborn as could be.

"You can do it, my big beautiful Babe!" Paul said.

Babe tried again. He strained so hard that his eyes nearly turned pink. He sweated so that water poured from the tips of his horns. He grunted and pulled, and his legs sank into the ground like mighty blue posts.

There was a snap, and then a loud C-R-A-C-K! Paul saw the first kink come out of the road, and he cheered. The road kept fighting back, flopping around and trying to hold on to its crooked twists and turns, but it was no match for Babe. At last, the road gave a kind of shiver and then lay still. Babe pulled it straighter than a railroad tie.

Paul Bunyan's chest swelled up so with pride that it broke one of his suspenders. The broken suspender whizzed up into the sky like a long rubber band. Just then, thousands of wild ducks were flying overhead. The suspender wrapped itself around the ducks and strangled the whole flock. Paul felt sorry for the ducks, but there was nothing to do but gather them up and hand them over to the cooks.

That night, after a wonderful duck dinner, Paul's bookkeeper John Inkslinger started writing down all that had happened. He was busily scratching away with his pen when he saw that he had only two barrels of ink left. He asked Paul what to do.

"That's easy," said Paul. "Don't bother to dot your *i*'s or cross your *t*'s. You'll save enough ink that way to get by until we can haul in another load of ink in the spring. Then you can fix up the *i*'s and *t*'s."

Winters could be very cold there in Wisconsin and Minnesota. One year, Lake Superior froze solid from top to bottom. In the spring, Paul had to haul all the ice out of the lake and stack it up on shore to thaw.

That same winter, men's words froze in front of their mouths and hung stiff in the air. Brimstone Bill, who was a great talker, was frozen in by a solid wall of words all turned to ice. Paul had to chip the ice from around Bill's shoulders, tie a rope to him, and have Babe pull him out.

The greatest logging job Paul ever did was in North Dakota, where some of the trees were so tall it took a man a whole day to see up to their tops. Shortly after Paul had finished logging off

18

most of the white pine, spruce, and hemlock in Minnesota, he received a letter from the King of Sweden. Paul's Swedish blacksmith Ole read the letter to Paul.

"The king says there are too many Swedes in Sweden. He wants to send a batch of them over here, but they need rich farmland without many trees, so they can raise wheat. He says he'll pay you in silver and gold if you can fix up a place for them."

Paul thought awhile, puffing on his pipe so hard that the sky began to cloud over. "North Dakota's the place," he said. "Nice and flat for farming. I'll fix it up for the Swedes, but I'm going to have to build the biggest logging camp ever built."

There never was such building, banging, tree-whacking, and hammering as went on in North Dakota when Paul started the new camp. Cook houses, bunk houses, and sheds grew up out of the ground, each building as big as a good-sized town. The dining room alone was so long that the man who brought the salt and pepper wagons around started out at one end in the morning and did not reach the other end until night.

Paul had found that it was easier to skid logs on roads made slippery with ice. There weren't many lakes in North Dakota, so Paul hauled his water for freezing from Lake Superior. He put the water into a big tank which Babe pulled. The thousands of lakes in Minnesota today were made by Babe's hoofs sinking into the ground and the holes filling up with water that leaked out of the tank. On one trip, Babe slipped and the tank tipped over. All the water ran out and started the Mississippi River.

On the day that Paul had cut down the last big tree in North Dakota, he stood looking around proudly. Then he frowned. Everywhere he looked there were hundreds and thousands of stumps sticking up. The Swedish farmers weren't going to like those stumps standing in the way of their plows.

"Blast it all!" Paul said, angry at himself for not having pulled the trees up roots and all. "Blast!" he thundered again and brought his fist whistling down on the stump beside him. The stump sank a foot below ground.

Paul Bunyan stared, scratched the side of his head, and stomped off to find Ole the blacksmith. "Ole," said Paul, "I want you to make me a maul—and make it as strong as Brimstone Bill's breath!"

The next morning, before the regular workday began, Paul went out with the new maul, which was like a giant hammer. He began knocking the stumps down into the ground. After about two weeks, working a couple of hours each morning, he had hammered every stump into the earth.

The King of Sweden was pleased when he heard about the fine job Paul had done, but one thing troubled him. He sent the Swedish ambassador to ask Paul if the soil in North Dakota was rich enough to grow fine crops.

"I'll prove that it is," said Paul. He got himself a kernel of corn, dug a hole four feet deep with a flick of his thumb, and dropped the corn in. "You come back in a week," he told the king's messenger, "and you'll see a fat stalk of corn pushing up out of the ground." He started to walk off, when he heard a rustling, whooshing sound behind him.

Paul turned. The kernel of corn had already sprouted and was rising up like a green rocket. In one minute it grew as high as Paul Bunyan's eyebrows. In two minutes more its tip struck a flying eagle and then split a cloud in two.

The Swedish ambassador's false teeth jumped out of his mouth and started biting the ground in excitement. "You'd better stop that corn growing!" he yelled at Paul. "It's apt to poke a hole in the sky and let all the air out. Besides, if I tell the king about it, he'll think it's just a tall story I made up."

Paul called to his men. "Ole," he said when all the men arrived, "you climb up there fast and cut the top off."

Ole straddled the stalk, but the thing was growing so fast it took Ole right along with it. Before Paul could think of what to do, Ole was out of sight.

"Come on down!" Paul yelled up at Ole.

Ole was almost beyond hearing then. When he answered, his voice took an hour to fall back to earth. "I can't come down! For every two feet I climb down, it carries me up ten!"

Paul bit the ends of his whiskers, rubbed his forehead, and tried to think of what to do. He ordered Shotgun Gunderson to load his rifle with doughnuts and sourdough bread and shoot it up to Ole so that Ole wouldn't starve to death while waiting for Paul to rescue him.

Finally, Paul took his biggest and brightest axe and began chopping at the base of the cornstalk. The stalk was growing so fast, he couldn't hit the same place twice with his axe. He put a chain around the stalk, planning to have Babe pull the corn out by its roots. The stalk grew out over the chain and pulled it into the air before Paul could even call Babe.

Paul remembered the iron rails that the men who had been building the Great Northern Railroad had left lying beside the tracks. He marched off a few miles, picked up an armload of the rails, and came back. He tied the rails together, wrapped them around the cornstalk, and made a tight knot. The cornstalk grew fatter and thicker. With every foot the stalk grew, the iron hoop around it sank in deeper.

"It's going to kill itself if it keeps on growing," said John Inkslinger. "It's going to cut itself in two."

That is what the cornstalk did. It gave a shudder at last and started to sway. It was so tall that it took three days to hit the ground. Just before it hit, Ole jumped off, so he fell only four feet and didn't get a scratch.

The Swedish ambassador wrote to the king that the soil seemed pretty rich, and the king sent Paul a shipload of money.

Paul began looking around for an even bigger job. Most of the land nearby had been logged over, and there weren't many large forests left. Paul decided to go west to the Pacific Ocean. There were trees there so huge, called the Big Trees, that it took a day to walk around them. There were redwood trees and Douglas fir trees so tall they were bent over from pressing against the sky.

Paul told his friends good-by, and he and Babe started out for the West Coast. On the way, Paul happened to let his peavey, a pole with a sharp spike on the end, drag along behind him. This made a rut that is now called the Grand Canyon. Farther on, heading through Oregon and Washington, Babe trampled some hills in the way, and that made the passes in the Cascade Mountains.

When Paul Bunyan started lumbering in the West, the fir and redwoods began to fall like grass. He built one big camp after another and invented all sorts of ways to make the lumbering business go faster. When the biggest part of the job was done, he grew restless again. He would go and sit on a hill with the Blue Ox and think about the old days. Even though there was gray in his beard now—and gray mixed in with the blue hairs on Babe's coat—Paul felt almost as young as ever.

"We've had a good life, eh, Blue Babe?"

Babe's soft blue eyes would shine, and he would push his damp muzzle against Paul Bunyan's cheek.

"Yes, sir, Babe, old friend," said Paul on one of those starlit nights with the wind crooning in the sugar pines, "it's too good a life to leave. So I guess we'll just keep on going as long as there's a toothpick of a tree left anywhere."

Apparently, that is what Paul Bunyan and his blue ox did. They just kept on going. The last time anyone saw them they were up in Alaska. And people there say, when the wind is right, they can still hear Paul whirling his sky-bright axe and sending the shout of "T-I-M-B-E-R-R-R!" booming across the air.

Coyote Cowboy

There aren't as many coyotes in Texas now as there were when Pecos Bill was born. But the ones that there are still do plenty of howling at night, sitting out under the sagebrush like thin, gray shadows, and pointing their noses at the moon.

Some of the cowboys around the Pecos River country claim that the oldest coyotes remember the time when Bill lived with them and are howling because they are lonesome for him. It's not often that coyotes have a boy grow up with them like one of their own family.

Pecos Bill

Bill was pretty unusual from the start. When he was only a few days old he raised such a fuss about having to drink ordinary milk that his mother had to go and take milk from a mountain lion who was raising baby cubs. Bill's mother was rather unusual in her own way. Before Bill was born, she drove off forty-five Indian warriors from the family's covered wagon with an old broom handle. So, borrowing milk from a wild mountain lion was no problem for her.

Bill had over a dozen older brothers and sisters for playmates, but they were ordinary boys and girls and no match for him. When Bill was two weeks old, his father found a half-grown bear and brought the bear home.

"You treat this bear nice, now," Bill's father said.

The bear didn't feel friendly and threatened to take a bite out of Bill. Bill wrestled the bear and tossed it around until the bear put its paws over its head and begged for mercy. Bill couldn't talk yet, but he patted the bear to show that he didn't have any hard feelings. After that, the bear followed Bill around like a big, flat-footed puppy.

Pecos Bill's father was one of the first settlers in the West. There was lots of room in Texas, with so much sky that it seemed as if there couldn't be any sky left over for the rest of the United States. There weren't many people, and it was lonesome country, especially on nights when the wind came galloping over the land, rattling the bear grass and the yucca plants and carrying the tangy smell of greasewood. However, Bill didn't feel lonely often, with all the raccoons, badgers, and jack rabbits he had for friends. Once he made the mistake of trying to pet a skunk. The skunk sprayed Bill with its strong scent. Bill's mother had to hang Bill on the clothesline for a week to let the smell blow off him.

Bill was a little over one year old when another family of pioneers moved into the country. The new family settled about fifty miles from where Bill's folks had built their homestead.

"The country's getting too crowded," said Bill's father. "We've got to move farther west."

So the family scrambled back into their big wagon and set out, the oxen puffing and snorting as they pulled the wagon toward the Pecos River. Bill was sitting in the rear of the wagon when it hit some rocks in a dry stream bed. There was a jolt, and Bill went flying out of the wagon. He landed so hard that the wind was knocked out of him and he couldn't even cry out to let his folks know. It might not have made any difference if he had, because all his brothers and sisters were making such a racket and the wagon wheels were creaking so loudly that no one could have heard him. In fact, with so many other children in the family besides Bill, it was four weeks before Bill's folks even missed him. Then, of course, it was too late to find him.

Young Bill sat there in the dry stream bed awhile, wondering what to do. Wherever he looked there was only the prairie and the sky, completely empty except for a sharp-shinned hawk floating overhead. Bill felt more lonely than he ever had in his life. Then, suddenly, he saw a pack of coyotes off in the distance, eating the remains of a dead deer. The coyotes looked at Bill, and Bill looked at them. These coyotes had never seen a human baby before, and they didn't know quite what to think. Apparently, they decided Bill was some new kind of hairless animal, for one of the female coyotes took a hunk of deer meat in her teeth and trotted over to Bill with it. She put it in front of him and stood back, waiting for him to eat it.

Bill had not eaten much raw meat before, but he knew that

26

the female coyote meant well, and he didn't want to hurt her feelings. So he picked the meat up and began chewing. It tasted so good that he walked over and joined the other coyotes.

From that time on, Bill lived with the coyotes, going wherever they went, joining in their hunts, and even learning their language. Those years he lived with the coyotes were happy ones. He ran with them through the moonlit nights, curled up with them in their shady dens, and howled with them when they sang to the stars.

By the time Bill was ten years old, he could out-run and out-howl any coyote in the Southwest. And since he had not seen any other human beings in all that time, he thought he was a coyote himself.

He might have gone on believing this forever if one day a cowboy hadn't come riding through the sagebrush. The cowboy stopped, stared, and rubbed his eyes, because he could scarcely believe what he saw. There in front of him stood a ten-year-old boy, as naked as a cow's hoof, wrestling with a giant grizzly bear. Nearby sat a dozen coyotes, their tongues hanging out. Before the cowboy could say, "Yipee yi-yo!" or plain "Yipee!" the boy had hugged the bear to death.

When Pecos Bill saw the cowboy, he snarled like a coyote and put his head down between his shoulders, ready to fight.

"What's your name?" the cowboy asked. "What are you doing out here?"

Since Bill didn't know anything but coyote talk, he naturally didn't understand a word.

The cowboy tossed Bill a plug of tobacco. Bill ate it and decided it tasted pretty good, so when the cowboy came up close, Bill didn't bite him.

The cowboy stayed there for three days, teaching Bill to talk like a human. Then he tried to prove to Bill that Bill wasn't a coyote.

"I must be a coyote," Bill said. "I've got fleas, haven't I? And I can howl the moon out of the sky. And I can run a deer to death."

"All Texans have got fleas and can howl," the cowboy said. "In order to be a true coyote, you have to have a bushy tail."

Bill looked around and realized for the first time that he didn't have a nice bushy, waving tail like his coyote friends. "Maybe I lost it somewhere."

"No siree," the cowboy said. "You're a human being, sure as shooting. You'd better come along with me."

Being human was a hard thing for Bill to face up to, but he realized that the cowboy must be right. He told his coyote friends good-by and thanked them for all that they had taught him. Then he straddled a mountain lion he had tamed and rode with the cowboy toward the cowboy's ranch. On the way to the ranch, a big rattlesnake reared up in front of them. The cowboy galloped off, but Bill jumped from his mount and faced the snake.

"I'll let you have the first three bites, Mister Rattler, just to be fair. Then I'm going to beat the poison out of you until you behave yourself!"

That is just what Bill did. He whipped the snake around until it stretched out like a thirty-foot rope. Bill looped the rattler-rope in one hand, got back on his lion, and caught up with the cowboy. To entertain himself, he made a loop out of the snake and tossed it over the head of an armadillo plodding along through the cactus. Next, he lassoed several Gila monsters.

"I never saw anybody do anything like that before," said the cowboy.

"That's because nobody invented the lasso before," said Pecos Bill.

Before Pecos Bill came along, cowboys didn't know much about their job. They didn't know anything about rounding up cattle, or branding them, or even about ten-gallon hats. The only way they knew to catch a steer was to hide behind a bush, lay a looped rope on the ground, and wait for the steer to step into the loop.

Pecos Bill changed all that the minute he reached the Dusty Dipper Ranch. He slid off his mountain lion and marched up to the biggest cowboy there.

"Who's the boss here?" he asked.

The man took one look at Bill's lion and at the rattlesnake rope, and said, "I *was*."

Young though he was, Bill took over. At the Dusty Dipper and at other ranches, Bill taught the cowboys almost everything they know today. He invented spurs for them to wear on their boots. He taught them how to round up the cattle and drive the herds to railroad stations where they could be shipped to market. One of the finest things Bill did was to teach the cowboys to sing cowboy songs.

Bill made himself a guitar. On a night when the moon was as reddish yellow as a ripe peach, though fifty times as large, he led some of the fellows at the ranch out to the corral and set himself down on the top rail.

"I don't want to brag," he told the cowhands, "but I learned my singing from the coyotes, and that's about the best singing there is."

He sang a tune the coyotes had taught him, and made up his own words:

"My seat is in the saddle, and my saddle's in the sky,
And I'll quit punchin' cows in the sweet by and by."

He made up many more verses and sang many other songs. When Bill was through, the roughest cowboy of all, Hardnose Hal, sat wiping tears from his eyes because of the beauty of Bill's singing. Lefty Lightning, the smallest cowboy, put his head down on his arms and wept. All the cowboys there vowed they would learn to sing and make up songs. And they did make up hundreds of songs about the lone prairie, and the Texas sky, and the wind blowing over the plains. That's why we have so many cowboy songs today.

Pecos Bill invented something else almost as useful as singing. This happened after a band of cattle rustlers came to the ranch and stole half a hundred cows.

"You boys," said Bill, "have to get something to protect yourselves with besides your fists. I can see I'll have to think up a six-shooter."

"What's a six-shooter?" asked Bronco-Busting Bertie. (Bill had taught horses how to buck and rear so that cowboys could learn bronco-busting.)

"Why," said Bill, "that's a gun that holds six bullets."

Bill sat down in the shade of a yucca tree and figured out how to make a six-shooter. It was a useful invention, but it had its bad side. Some of the cowboys started shooting at each other. Some even went out and held up trains and stage coaches.

One of the most exciting things Bill did was to find himself the wildest, strongest, most beautiful horse that ever kicked up the Texas dust. He was a mighty, golden mustang, and even Bill couldn't outrun that horse. To catch the mustang, Bill had the cowboys rig up a huge slingshot and shoot him high over the cactus and greasewood. When Bill landed in front of the mustang, the horse was so surprised he stopped short, thrusting out his front legs stiff as rifle barrels. The mustang had been going so fast that his hoofs drove into the ground, and he was stuck. Bill leaped on the animal's back, yanked on his golden mane, and pulled him free. The mustang was so thankful for being pulled from the trap that he swung his head around and gave Pecos Bill a smacking kiss. From then on, the horse was as gentle as a soft wind in a thatch of Jimson weed.

No one else could ride him, however. Most of the cowboys who tried ended up with broken necks. That's why Bill called his mustang Widow-Maker.

Bill and Widow-Maker traveled all over the western range, starting new ranches and helping out in the long cattle drives. In stormy weather they often holed up with a band of coyotes. Bill would strum his guitar and the coyotes would sing with him.

Then came the year of the Terrible Drought. The land shriveled for lack of water, and the droves of cattle stood panting with thirst.

The cowboys and the ranch bosses from all around came to Bill, saying, "The whole country's going to dry up and blow away, Bill, unless you can figure out some way to bring us rain."

"I'm figuring," Bill told them. "But I've never tried making rain before, so I'll have to think a little."

While Bill thought, the country grew so dry it seemed that there would be nothing but bones and rocks left. Even cactus plants, which could stand a lot of dryness, began to turn brown. The pools where the cattle drank dried up and turned to cracked mud. The sun was redder than a whole tribe of painted

Indians. All the snakes hid under the ground in order to keep from frying. Even the coyotes stopped howling, because their throats were too dry for them to make any sound.

Bill rode around on Widow-Maker, watching the clear, burning sky and hoping for the sight of a rain cloud. All he saw were whirls of dust, called dust devils, spinning up from the yellowing earth. Then, toward noon one day, he spied something over in Oklahoma which looked like a tall whirling tower of black bees.

Widow-Maker reared up on his hind legs, his eyes rolling.

"It's just a cyclone," Pecos Bill told his horse, patting the golden neck.

But Widow-Maker was scared and began bucking around so hard that even Bill had a time staying in the saddle.

"Whoa there!" Bill commanded. "I could ride that cyclone as easy as I can ride you, the way you're carrying on."

That's when Bill had an idea. There might be rain mixed up in that cyclone tower. He nudged Widow-Maker with his spurs and yelled, "Giddap!"

What Bill planned to do was leap from his horse and grab the cyclone by the neck. But as he came near and saw how high the top of the whirling tower was, he knew he would have to do something better than that. Just as he and Widow-Maker came close enough to the cyclone to feel its hot breath, a knife of lightning streaked down into the ground. It stuck there, quivering, just long enough for Bill to reach out and grab it. As the lightning bolt whipped back up into the sky, Bill held on. When he was as high as the top of the cyclone, he jumped and landed astraddle its black, spinning shoulders.

By then, everyone in Texas, New Mexico, Arizona, and Oklahoma was watching. They saw Bill grab hold of that cyclone's shoulders and haul them back. They saw him wrap his legs around the cyclone's belly and squeeze so hard the cyclone started to pant. Then Bill got out his lasso and slung it around the cyclone's neck. He pulled it tighter and tighter until the cyclone started to choke, spitting out rocks and dust. All the rain that was mixed up in it started to fall.

Down below, the cattle and the coyotes, the jack rabbits and the horned toads, stuck out their tongues and caught the sweet, blue, falling rain. Cowboys on the ranches and people in town ran around whooping and cheering, holding out pans and kettles to catch the raindrops.

Bill rode the cyclone across three states. By the time the cyclone reached California, it was all out of steam, and out of rain, too. It gave a big sigh, trembled weakly, and sank to earth. Bill didn't have time to jump off. He fell hard, scooping out a few thousand acres of sand and rock and leaving a big basin below sea level. That was what made Death Valley.

Bill was a greater hero than ever after that. Yet at times, he felt almost as lonely as on the day when he had bounced out of his folks' wagon and found himself sitting alone under the empty sky. Widow-Maker was good company most of the time, but Bill felt there was something missing in his life.

One day, he wandered down to the Rio Grande and stood watching the brown river flow slowly past. Suddenly, he saw a catfish as big as a whale jumping around on top of the water, its whiskers shining like broomsticks. On top of the catfish was a brown-eyed, brown-haired girl.

Somebody beside Bill exclaimed, "Look at Slue-Foot Sue ride that fish!"

Pecos Bill felt his heart thump and tingle in a way it had never done before. "That's the girl I want to marry!" he said. He waded out into the Rio Grande, poked the catfish in the nose, and carried Slue-Foot Sue to a church. "You're going to be my bride," he said.

"That's fine with me," said Sue, looking Pecos Bill over and seeing that he was the biggest, boldest, smartest cowboy who had ever happened to come along beside the Rio Grande.

That was the beginning of a very happy life for Bill. He and Sue raised a large family. All of the boys grew up to be fine cowboys, and the girls grew up to be cowgirls. The only time

Bill and Sue had any trouble was when Bill wanted to adopt a batch of baby coyotes who were orphans.

"We're human beings," Sue said, "and we can't be raising a bunch of varmints."

"I was a varmint once myself," said Bill. He argued so much that Sue agreed to take the coyotes in and raise them as members of the family. The coyotes grew to be so human that two of them were elected to the House of Representatives.

Pecos Bill grew old, as everyone and everything does in time. Even so, there wasn't a bronco he couldn't bust, or a steer he couldn't rope, or a bear he couldn't hug to death faster and better than anyone else.

No one knows, for sure, how he died, or even if he did die. Some say that he mixed barbed wire in his coffee to make it strong enough for his taste, and that the wire rusted in his stomach and poisoned him. Others say that one day he met a dude cowboy, all dressed up in fancy clothes, who didn't know the front end of a cow from the side of a boxcar. The dude asked so many silly questions about cow punching that Pecos Bill lay down in the dust and laughed himself to death.

But the cowboys back in the Pecos River country say that every once in a while, when the moon is full and puffing its white cheeks out and the wind is crooning softly through the bear grass, Pecos Bill himself comes along and sits on his haunches and sings right along with the coyotes.

Five Fathoms Tall

No one knows exactly where Alfred Bulltop Stormalong came from, though most people agree it was a place with "nuck" or "nocket" or "tucket" on the end. Massachusetts has a number of towns and islands with names ending that way. Nantucket, Nantasket, Squibnocket, and Tuckernuck are a few. These are all sea-touched places, and since Stormalong was a great seaman, he may have been born in Massachusetts.

Wherever it was, the ocean was right next door, booming and bouncing against the shore and sending salt spray over everything. Stormalong breathed in so much of the spray that there was ocean water in his veins. He watched the waves so often that his eyes, which were brown at first, changed to the blue-gray color of the sea. Most of all, he liked to watch the ships sailing toward the ports of New England's coast. Before he even knew how to talk, Stormy could tell a frigate from a brigantine and could tie sailor's knots in the yarn his mother made on her spinning wheel. The moment he did begin to talk, he told his mother he wanted to be a sailor.

"There have been enough sailors in the family," his mother said. "If your father had stayed on shore, I wouldn't be a widow." She had to tip her head back quite a way to look up at her son because Stormy was growing so fast. "It's time someone stayed home and kept his feet dry," she said.

Stormalong hadn't learned enough words yet to be able to argue, so he went out and played in the sand. Far off on the curving blue of the horizon was a white-sailed sloop, its keel plowing up the waves like snow drifts. Stormalong made a hill of sand and climbed up on it to get a better look. The sand hill was so high and Stormalong was so tall that the sloop's captain changed course, thinking Stormalong was a new lighthouse.

By the time Stormy was ten years old, he was already two fathoms high. A fathom is about six feet, so Stormy was pretty tall.

His mother found him one day sitting with his chin on his fist, looking worried.

"Are you sick, Stormy?" she asked, stretching up to pat his knee.

"No, I'm thinking that maybe there aren't any ships big enough to take me on as a cabin boy."

"Can't you think of anything except seafaring?"

"No," Stormy said.

A couple of years later, his yearning for a boat of his own was so strong that he started to make one. Near the beach there was a big, old house that no one seemed to own. He picked it up and turned it upside down in the water, thinking that he would put a sail and a rudder on it. The roof was so leaky that the ocean came pouring up through it, and the house sank before Stormy could count to ten.

"Where's the Mason house?" his mother asked a few hours later.

"It sank," Stormalong told her. "I was trying to make a boat out of it."

"Oh, dear!" his mother cried. "Some new people just bought it to fix up for a seaside home. Now what shall we do?"

"I'd better hurry off to sea before the new people get here," Stormy said.

For once, his mother did not argue. She fixed him a small, hundred-pound bundle of food and polished the buttons on his pea jacket. Then she climbed up the ladder kept for the purpose and kissed him good-by.

Stormalong headed toward Boston, where there were more ships than seagulls. He hadn't been on the wharves long when he heard that the owner of a schooner called the *Silver Maid* was signing up sailors for a voyage to China.

Stormalong marched up to the captain and said, "I'd like to sign on as cabin boy."

The captain tipped his head back until he spotted where Stormy's voice was coming from. "How old are you, sonny?"

"They tell me I'm about thirteen," Stormy said. "Maybe that's a little young, but I'm getting older every day."

"Have you ever been to sea before?"

"No, sir," said Stormy, "but all the Stormalongs have been seafaring people."

"Are you strong and healthy?"

"I had the colic once when I was a baby, from drinking too many barrels of milk," said Stormy. "Excuse me a minute. The topsail on your mizzenmast seems a mite crooked." He reached up easily and straightened the sail.

The captain stared so hard he nearly lost his eyesight. When he could see again, he tapped the ledger on his desk and said, "Sign here, lad."

Stormy took a pen and wrote down his last name, "Stormalong." After it, he wrote his initials, "A. B."

The ship's mate walked over. He gazed up at Stormalong and said to the captain, "He looks like an able-bodied seaman, right enough." Then he glanced at the page where Stormy had written his name. "I guess that's what the initials of this name stand for—*Seaman, Able-Bodied.*"

After Stormy had been on the *Silver Maid* a few days, the rest of the sailors agreed that he was about as able-bodied as any seaman they had ever shipped with. The first-class seamen among them decided to put "A. B." after their own names when they signed any ship's papers, and sailors have continued to do so to this day.

Stormalong still had a few things to learn, such as being careful not to stand too close to the ship's rail. His weight would make the ship list until it was in danger of sinking. When it was his turn to polish the deck and the brasses, he took pains not to scrub too hard for fear he would scrub the whole ship out from under the crew. He had to sleep in an extra-large lifeboat because there wasn't a sailor's hammock half large enough to hold him.

Stormalong

In spite of his being a bit clumsy and singing sea chanteys so loudly that it took three dozen other sailors to sing a duet with him, young Stormalong was as popular a cabin boy as ever went to sea. He was popular with everyone except the cook. It was hard for a growing boy to curb his appetite so that the ship's supply of salt pork, jerked beef, and molasses would last until the *Silver Maid* reached China. Stormy could eat a boatload of eggs, plus the hens who had laid them, for breakfast.

The ship churned along toward China with a cargo of furs and hides and ginseng roots, to exchange for tea, raw silk, and sweet-smelling spices. Stormy was happier than a porpoise until one day the *Silver Maid* stopped with a sudden jar. The wind was blowing, the sails were full, but the ship stood rock-still in mid-ocean.

One of Stormy's shipmates turned pale and shouted, "A kraken's got hold of the keel!"

"What's a kraken?" asked Stormy.

"I hardly dare to tell you, lad," said the sailor. "It's something like an octopus, only it has more arms. It's like a crab, but it bites ten times as hard. It has jaws that can snap a mast in two. It can turn a ship into splinters and hold it standing still in a typhoon. It's the fiercest, cruelest, most powerful and pitiless monster an able-bodied seaman can ever meet!"

The captain came on deck, wringing his hands. "Men," he called, "I want a volunteer to dive overboard and see what's holding us back. Step forward, somebody."

All the men except Stormalong took two steps backward.

"I'd be proud to take a look, Captain," said Stormalong. "Maybe I'd better stick a knife in my belt, though, in case whatever it is down there won't let go without an argument."

"Bring the gallant boy a knife!" the captain ordered.

The cook rushed forward with a chopping cleaver. Stormy pushed it under his belt, climbed up on the bowsprit, and dived into the water.

The farther down he went, the darker it became. The water changed from blue to dark weedy green to blackish purple. Stormy was well down below the ship's keel when he saw a long claw-like arm reaching up out of the blackness. The claw end had hold of the ship, and all the suckers along the arm were hanging on to the tide so tightly, even the tide was standing still. Then, way down toward the basement of the ocean, Stormy saw an eye staring up at him. The eye belonged to a strange head from which a dozen other arms grew.

If it isn't a kraken, thought Stormy, it's something worse. He pulled the cleaver from his belt and started whacking at the claw-like arm holding on to the ship. His blade bounced off the arm like rubber. He tried harder and finally slashed through. At once, two more arms appeared and took an even firmer grip on the ship's keel.

Stormalong felt somewhat discouraged until he had a thought. He tossed his cleaver away and grabbed hold of one of the slippery arms. He wound his fingers around it. He pulled and yanked. The claw lost its hold. Stormy started twisting the arm into a figure-of-eight knot. Next, he grabbed the second arm and tied it into a fisherman's bend. Immediately, the monster fastened extra arms to the schooner. Stormalong wrestled each one of them and tied more knots than had even been invented. Finally, the monster was so tangled up, it slithered away and drowned in its own sweat.

A few sharks gathered around, sniffing for blood. Stormalong simply kicked them out of his way and swam to the surface. He expected to find everything peaceful. Instead, waves were dashing against the ship like green mountains, and sailors were scrambling through the rigging to lash the sails.

Realizing that it was his fight undersea which had caused the tempest, Stormalong crawled on deck as gently as he could. The captain was so delighted with the rescue of the ship that he asked Stormy to sign on right then for the next trip.

Stormalong thought awhile, and then he said, "Maybe I'm a little too big for a schooner like this. Anyhow, I think I'll take a short vacation after this trip and go help John Paul Jones finish off the American Revolution."

According to some stories, Stormalong did exactly that and was at the side of John Paul Jones when the *Bon Homme Richard* defeated the English ship *Serapis*.

Others say that Stormalong couldn't find a ship large enough for himself, and deciding that his mother had been right all along, he became a farmer. There may be some truth in this, for about that time there was a potato farmer by the name of A. B. Stormalong, way out in the Northwest Territory. Farmer Stormalong became famous, because during a terrible dry spell he managed to grow a wonderful crop by working so hard that his own sweat watered the potato plants.

But it wasn't long before Stormy turned up on the sea again, this time as a boatswain, a superior seaman in charge of rigging, cables, cordage, and the like. He was a strapping young man by then, taller than a whale standing on end. Even though he had outgrown his boyish clumsiness, he felt pretty cramped on even the biggest ships the American dockyards put out.

"I'll build me a clipper ship my size," Stormalong finally decided, and he went to work with the help of a few thousand shipyard workers. The work continued for nearly three years. So much wood went into the clipper ship that there was a lumber shortage over the entire country. The sails alone were so huge the sailmakers had to go to the Sahara Desert in order to find room enough to cut and sew them. The masts were high enough to scrape the sun and graze the moon. Stormalong solved that problem by putting hinges on the masts so that they could be lowered. Even then, the ship knocked a few silver chips from low-hanging stars.

Stormalong named his clipper the *Courser*. All clipper ships were built for speed, but the *Courser* was the fastest of all, especially when Stormy stood at the pilot's wheel. He could whirl the wheel around with one finger, though it took thirty-three regular sailors to do the job, even on a calm sea.

Stormalong carried cargoes all over the world, to China, India, and Europe, but no harbor anywhere was large enough for the *Courser*. Stormalong had to anchor far offshore and then have a fleet come to take the cargo to land.

One time, Stormalong had a shipload of coffee and soap to deliver to Norway. The shortest route to Norway was through the English Channel.

"We shouldn't have much trouble getting through the Channel," he told one of his fifty officers, "but I'm a shade worried about the Strait of Dover. It's only twenty-one miles wide between the cliffs and the French coast."

As the *Courser* neared the strait, Stormalong called his sailors together, a thousand of them in all. Because the ship was so long, it took half a day for the message to travel from bow to stern.

Stormy told the crew, "I want five hundred of you to carry slabs of soap on deck. The other five hundred go over the side in lifeboats and start slicking that soap onto the ship. Put it on thick from stem to stern."

The sailors went to work. When they were through, the *Courser*'s sides were so slippery with white soap that even the barnacles lost their grip and slid off. Stormalong steered the ship forward. Ahead, the cliffs of Dover rose blackly against the sky.

All the men stiffened in fear as the captain sent the clipper edging through the narrow gap. There was a scraping noise as the left side of the *Courser* brushed against the cliffs. Stormalong put both hands on the wheel, his face grim. There could be no turning back.

The ship went scraping and rubbing along, and it was only because of the soap on its sides that it got through. Naturally, much of the soap rubbed off on the cliffs, turning them white. They have been called the white cliffs of Dover ever since.

Stormalong decided that perhaps his ship was a mite too big for ordinary trade, and he was growing bored with carrying ordinary things like coffee, soap, and lumber.

Stormalong put his fist under his chin one day and tried to think of big kinds of cargo.

Just then, off on the horizon something reared up. Stormalong caught a glimpse of a huge, sleek, brine-dripping back. A great flashing tail slapped downward and shook the ocean. A plume of whitish mist soared upward.

"Whales!" Stormalong exclaimed. "That's it!"

Stormalong turned the *Courser* into a whaling ship and set out to chase and harpoon every big-jawed, small-eyed, snorting and cavorting whale from the poles to the equator. In those early days of America, people wanted all the things which could be made from whales, such as oil and corsets and even perfume. Year after year, Captain Stormalong sent his clipper racing after whales of every kind—white whales, gray whales,

finbacks, humpbacks, sperm whales, and especially blue whales, the biggest whales of all.

Until Stormalong's time, whaleboats had to draw dangerously close to a whale before the man holding a harpoon could sink the sharp point into the creature. Even the best harpoonists could throw the spear little farther than thirty feet. Stormalong practiced harpoon throwing until he could hit a whale even before it swam up over the horizon. If the whale didn't measure at least a hundred feet long, Stormalong would toss it back into the ocean.

If a whale weighed only ninety tons, he would say, "That's robbing the cradle. I'd better let that poor, puny little spouter grow up a bit more."

Some of the best whaling grounds were in the arctic regions, but ships were often crushed by the ice. Stormalong could shove icebergs back with a push of one hand, or chip enough ice off an ice wall to freeze a whole whale in the *Courser*'s icehouse. By doing this, Stormalong became the inventor of the first refrigerator ship.

Stormalong never enjoyed anything quite so much as whaling. This was partly because he loved to eat whale steaks. He had a dozen cooks on board to cook all the whale steak and shark soup he wanted and a crew of helpers to rush the food to him in wheelbarrows. After he had eaten and had drunk a few barrels of apple cider, which gushed down to him through a fire hose, he would stretch out on deck and pick his teeth with a marlinespike or an oar.

There was only one thing that worried Stormy, and that was the way steamships were beginning to appear on the high seas. The steamships grew larger and faster with every year that passed. Finally, one of them actually sped past the mighty *Courser*. When that happened, Stormalong bellowed in such anger that he blew his own beard off.

The ship which beat the *Courser* was a swift, powerful packet ship from Liverpool, England. Stormy was determined to have another race with the *Liverpool Packet,* and win. He spent so much time watching for the other ship to come within racing range again that whales as big as thunderheads moved past the *Courser* without his even noticing. Then one calm day, the English ship came steaming toward him, on her way to Boston.

"I'll beat you to Boston, or die trying!" Stormalong yelled across to the British captain. "Just give me a good wind."

"We don't need wind," the other captain shouted. "We've a hold full of coal, and boilers full of steam." The packet pulled ahead, leaving the *Courser* sitting helplessly behind on a wind-less sea.

Two days passed and Stormalong's great clipper stood as still as a painting. Then at dawn on the third day, the sails fluttered. In ten minutes more, they shook. In another ten minutes, a hurricane wind was blasting through the rigging, tearing at the sails and making the masts sway like seaweed.

"Reef the sails!" the first mate cried at Stormy. "The wind will tear them to ribbons." Even as he spoke, a mizzenmast cracked and broke, dragging down enough canvas to cover a city.

Stormalong said only, "Full sail ahead! I asked for wind and it's here. I'll be in Boston so far ahead of that packet ship, the *Liverpool*'s crew will die of old age before they catch up." He took a firmer grip on the pilot wheel and steered ahead.

The sails rattled as if they were made of dry leaves. The timbers of the ship groaned and trembled. Waves taller than the tallest trees broke over the plunging prow.

The foresails split. The wind sliced them as if with knives.

"Captain!" the first mate yelled again above the storm. "Take in the sails, or we'll go to the bottom."

Stormalong wrapped both arms around the shaking wheel. His face was pale, and his eyes were the color of icebergs. "Full sail ahead!" he roared.

That afternoon, the *Courser* whooshed past the *Liverpool Packet*. Soon the packet ship was left behind, looking no larger than a canoe on the horizon. Stormalong took a deep breath of spray and closed his eyes, smiling, feeling the wind gust against his cheeks.

In his mind, he dreamed of a ship so large only the sky would be roomy enough for it. He would go sailing around the sun and the planets, and throw a harpoon into the Big Dipper just for fun.

The next morning the people at Provincetown saw a giant ghostly ship scud across Massachusetts Bay. Its sails were splinters of cloth and most of its masts were broken. But it was not until the *Courser* reached Boston, hours ahead of the *Liverpool Packet,* that people saw the great lifeless figure slumped over the pilot's wheel.

Some people say that wasn't the end of Stormalong. They say he did go on to build a great ship in the sky, and that it is the ship's shadow which causes the eclipse of the moon. They say he's hunting sky whales up there, and that when shooting stars fall to earth, they have been knocked out of the sky by Stormalong's harpoon.

Mike Fink

River Roarer

The Mississippi and the Missouri rivers are usually pretty quiet these days. It was a lot different when Mike Fink was whooping up and down them in his keelboat. But then, Mike was about the noisiest thing next to thunder that this country has ever heard.

Mike was born to be a riverman, although he didn't know it until he was old enough to find out. Until then he spent his time in the woods around Pittsburgh, where he was born, shooting at wolves, bobcats, mosquitoes, or anything else that could be shot at. He wasn't especially big, but he was as tough as a bale of barbed wire and as touchy as dynamite.

Even the wild Indians took a different path when they saw young Mike coming. He could flip a tomahawk through the air and hit a fly, even if the fly was in a hurry. With his rifle, called Bang-All, he could straighten out the curl in a pig's tail from fifty feet away.

Mike was as good at bragging as he was at shooting and fighting. "I can shoot faster than greased lightning going through a slippery thundercloud!" Mike boasted when he was still only ten years old. "I can shoot all the scales off a leaping trout with one bullet."

People who didn't know Mike too well laughed.

"I'll prove it!" Mike said. He jumped into the air, clapped his heels together, yelled "Cock-a-doodle-doo!" and loaded his long flintlock rifle at the same time. "Hold on to your hats and beards while I find something worth shooting at," he said.

"Farmer Neal's having a big shooting contest next Sunday," a townsman told him. "If you can shoot as well as you claim, you'll win a nice hunk of fresh beef. But you'll have to pay a quarter for each shot you try."

Mike went off and sharpened up his shooting eye by practicing on the wolves skulking around the woods near his family's log cabin. The wolves were low-slung, shifty fellows, hunting for a farmer's fat duck or even a skinny chicken. The government paid money for wolfskins, because wolves were a nuisance to the settlers. Mike banged and boomed at the wolves until he had about fifty skins. He took the skins to town and got enough money to enter the shooting match.

On Sunday, Mike dressed up in his best buckskin, stuck a wild-turkey feather in his cap, and marched off to Farmer

Neal's place. The silver trimmings on his rifle stock were polished like glass.

At the shooting contest, the field was crowded with people. The men trying for the prize were soldiers and hunters, Indian scouts and boatmen, all of them the best shots in the country. They grinned and winked at seeing young Mike there, and one said:

"You'd better let me lift you up so you can see the target, sonny."

"I can jump higher than a Plymouth Rock rooster and yell louder," Mike said. He gave a loud crow, jumped, waved his heels, and fired at a passing bee. The bee flipped over, closed its eyes, and landed at Mike's feet. But in a second, the bee sat up and buzzed.

"You didn't kill that bee, young fellow," a man said.

"Didn't plan to," Mike said and held up the bee. "I just snipped off his stinger so he won't bother me when I'm aiming at the target."

Everyone was silent after that, though each really believed Mike had been merely lucky. When his turn came, Mike stepped up to the firing line and got set to take his first shot. The target was a round, white piece of paper tacked to a board on a distant oak tree. At the very center of the paper was a small circle called the bull's-eye.

No one had hit the center of the white circle yet. Mike pulled the trigger. Bang-All banged, and the bullet zipped straight through the bull's-eye.

People whistled in surprise, but one man said, "I'll bet you can't do that again, sonny."

Mike blew the smoke from the muzzle of Bang-All. "I paid for five shots," he said, "and I'll drive every bullet right on top of the other, even with a blindfold on. For I can out-shoot, out-thunder, and out-lick any man, mountain lion, or war-whooping redskin this side of the Alleghenies, and the other side too!"

"Move the target farther back!" somebody yelled.

The target was moved so far off that some of the older people in the crowd started hunting for spyglasses in order to see it. Mike whipped his second bullet through the heart of the target. He sent his third bullet whamming in on top of the one before. When he had hit the bull's-eye five times, the rest of the marksmen decided they might as well go home and take up knitting.

Mike went home, too, lugging five quarters of beef with him. The Fink family had enough chops and roasts for a whole winter, even though Mike could eat a dozen steaks all by himself for breakfast.

At other shooting contests after that, the rival sharpshooters would give Mike a quarter of beef beforehand if he would promise not to take part. So Mike had to be satisfied with roaming in the woods, scouting for Indians. He wanted to join George Washington's army and fight the English in the American Revolution, but he was still a little too young to be a soldier.

With plenty of free meat, plus hominy and fried cornmeal and buckets of molasses, Mike grew stronger than ever, though he never grew overly tall. When he was seventeen, he started hanging around the river docks in Pittsburgh, watching the boats. There were barges and keelboats, flatboats and Indian canoes, and a few ships left over from the Revolutionary Navy. Some craft carried cargoes of flour, cloth, lumber, and nails. Some carried people and livestock from one town to another, for there were not many roads through the wilderness then.

Mike leaned on his six-foot-long rifle and dreamed about becoming a boatman. He watched the water churn against the sides of the river craft, sparkling like soapsuds. Best of all, he liked watching the men who ran the boats. Most of them were as powerful and as full of brag and fight as he was. A few wore red feathers in their hats. A red feather meant that the person wearing it was the roughest, toughest, hardest-to-beat riverman around.

"I aim to get me a red feather," Mike decided. "I aim to get me all the red feathers there are, from here to the Rockies, and on the other side, too!"

Mike told his folks good-by, polished up Bang-All until it glittered like a hive of bees, and walked up to the first keelboat captain he found in Pittsburgh.

"What can you do?" the captain asked Mike.

"There's just about nothing I can't do," said Mike, "except possibly drink up the Pacific Ocean in one swallow. Otherwise, I can out-roar a mother hurricane and all her family, knock down a thunderbolt with my breath, spit the Sahara Desert into a flood, and in my spare time, haul up so many whales, the Atlantic will sink a hundred feet. I can also do a few other things that I can't even think of right at the moment."

"I'll try you out," said the captain, and he wrote Mike's name down on the crew list.

Mike bought himself a proper keelboatman's outfit—a red shirt, blue jacket, linsey-woolsey pants, moccasins, a fur cap, and a wide belt from which he hung a knife. He strutted on board and looked around until he saw a big-nosed man with a red feather stuck in his cap. Mike swaggered over to the man, doubled up his fists, and roared:

"Whoop, hi-ho, and cock-a-doodle-do! I'm the original Pittsburgh screamer, weaned on shark's milk, raised in a crib with rattlesnakes, mad scorpions, and hungry bumblebees. I'm second cousin to a hurricane, first cousin to a seven-day blizzard, and brother to an earthquake! I'm so all-fired ferocious and ornery, it scares even me to think about it! And I'm so chock-full of fight and fury, I have to lick somebody or my muscles will bust like cannon balls!"

The big-nosed boatman, whose name was Carpenter, puffed up his chest and roared right back at Mike, "Whoop and holler! I'm a man-eating panther, with teeth like buzz saws and eyes sharp enough to bore holes through midnight. My mother was a tiger, and my father was a rhinoceros. I can crack an elephant's bones in one hand, break five grizzly bears' backs with the other, and blow down a forest with one breath. I'm so rough I don't dare scratch myself for fear my skin will come off!"

There was nothing to do but fight to prove who was the better man. The rest of the keelboatmen watched and trembled. The boat itself trembled as Mike and Carpenter wrestled and

writhed, struck and staggered, panted and puffed. They fought for two hours, sweating so hard that a crew of men had to bail the boat out to keep everyone from drowning. Finally, Mike gave a whoop loud enough to tear a hole through the boat deck, leaped, drove his feet into Carpenter's belly, and knocked Carpenter flat as a pancake turner.

Carpenter lay still. He said, "Whoop," but his voice was so weak that a ladybug sitting right on his chin couldn't hear it. When he gained enough strength, he stood up and gave Mike the red feather from his hat.

"Mike Fink," he said, "you're the best fighter on the Ohio, the Mississippi, the Missouri, and any other river in the U.S. of A."

"I don't want to brag," Mike said, "but I guess I am." He put the feather in his cap and shook Carpenter's hand.

The two felt so friendly that they promised they would die for each other, if they absolutely had to.

In between fighting and friendship-making, which amounted to the same thing, Mike learned how to be a regular keelboatman. He learned how to ram a long pole down to the bottom of the river and push the boat upstream against the current. He learned to watch out for sandbars or snags that could stop the boat. He could see a dead tree floating in the water almost before it died and dropped there.

Mike became the best keelboatman anywhere. Up and down the rivers he went, from Pittsburgh to St. Louis and to New Orleans. He could load up a boat with cargo in less time than it took the other boatmen to drink a cup of hard cider, and usually they drank so fast, they swallowed before they even got the cider to their mouths. Mike himself could drink so fast that he only swallowed in between two-gallon sips.

Mike Fink

By the time Mike had been on the river awhile, he had so many red feathers in his cap that he threw most of them away, for fear people would think he was a bonfire.

There were lazy times on the river, too, when Mike and his friend Carpenter would stretch out on the deck and watch the sun go by, or fish for catfish, or sit on shore at night studying a campfire.

On one of those lazy days, Mike felt the need for a little extra target practice. He took a tin cup full of cider, handed it to Carpenter, and said, "Pace off about sixty yards and set that cup on your head. I'll shoot it off."

Carpenter looked a bit nervous, but he did as he was told. Mike aimed Bang-All and fired. The bullet whistled through the cup's brim, not spilling a drop. Carpenter took his turn with the same trick. He hit the cup on Mike's head, but he spilled the cider.

From then on, Mike and Carpenter would show off their trick to all the other boatmen. One time, before Mike could fire at the cup on Carpenter's head, there was a blast from another rifle in the woods nearby. The cup flew into the air.

Mike spun around so fast the ground smoked. "Who did that?" he roared.

"My name's Talbot," a man said, stepping out of the woods. He was a red-headed fellow with muscles bunched up as thick as thunderclouds.

"Whoop, holler, and hailstones!" Mike yelled, jumping into the air and banging his heels together. "My name's cholera, pestilence, and sudden death! I'm the original meat-grinder, man-mauler, muscle-ripper, and the meanest, cruelest, blood-thirstiest creation that ever drew breath!"

Talbot took a deep breath and shouted back, "Whoop! I'm

the man who invented fighting. I've got fists so big they make mountains look like bumps. I've got a hide like an alligator and a heart as black as a buzzard in a coal mine! I'm so mean, I hate not being able to kill a man more than once!"

They leaped at each other. They hissed and hollered. They slammed, rolled, and punched. The ground shook, and the trees shook until all the leaves fell off. At last, after several hours, Mike swung his fist up from the ground. His knuckles banged Talbot's chin so hard that Talbot flew up and hit his head on a tree branch. When he sailed down to earth again, his head was considerably flatter, and all the fight had gone out of him.

Talbot and Mike shook hands, and when the men went back onto the keelboat, Talbot went along. He, Carpenter, and Mike all swore they would die for each other, if they absolutely had to.

With three mighty men like that fighting for each other and whooping up and down the rivers, it seemed there was no one they couldn't lick. But there was. The man who had them licked wasn't even very good with his fists, and he didn't whoop and holler at all. His name was Robert Fulton, and all he did to become the new ruler of the river was invent the steamboat.

Mike hated steamboats even more than he hated to sit still. Every time he saw one coming, its big side-wheels churning the water, he shook his fists at the sky. But the steamboats kept on coming, getting bigger and faster, pushing the keelboats out of the way, and winning every race.

Mike still worked on the keelboats, but it wasn't like the old days. He wasn't the real boss of the river anymore. And Pittsburgh, St. Louis, and New Orleans were growing too civilized for his liking.

That's how Mike happened to become a mountain man. Talbot and Carpenter did, too. In St. Louis one day, they signed up with a fur-trapping party to go up the Missouri River, farther west than almost anyone but Lewis and Clark had been before. They went in two keelboats loaded down with traps, guns, and supplies.

The Missouri was muddier than the underside of a mud turtle. It was so full of snags, the men used axes more than they used oars. The wild animals and Indians swarmed around the river banks in such numbers that Mike's rifle barrel grew so hot from shooting, it nearly melted.

"Come on, mountains!" Mike would roar, beating his chest. "Come on, you beaver and buffalo and grizzlies! I'm the original mountain-beater and grizzly-tamer, and I can out-trap, out-skin, and out-trade any man west or east of the sun!"

Mike turned out to be almost as good a trapper as he had been a riverman. That first winter, near the mouth of the Yellowstone River, he brought in so many furs that half the beaver population was left running around naked.

Mike was mighty happy and proud those days, and it seemed he could beat the Rockies down with his fists the way he claimed he could. But then he and his friend Carpenter had a quarrel. They whooped and hollered at each other and almost had a fist fight before they remembered that they were supposed to be friends. They made up and shook hands, but Mike didn't seem quite so hearty about it as usual.

Spring came to Fort Henry, the main camp. The men felt like celebrating, so they tuned up their banjos and blew the frost out of their harmonicas.

"Let's give them a show," Mike said to Carpenter. "We'll show them what real shooting's like." He handed Carpenter a cup of cider for Carpenter to place on his head.

Carpenter walked off sixty yards, put the cup on his head, and faced Mike. Some people say Carpenter trembled and didn't trust Mike, because of the quarrel. Others say he was as calm as a fence post on a windless day.

Mike brought Bang-All up against his cheek and squinted. For the first time in his life he had trouble holding the barrel steady. And the sunlight, glancing along the muzzle, made him blink. He shook himself, squeezed the trigger, and fired.

Carpenter gave a surprised look and fell, a bullet hole gleaming in the middle of his forehead.

"You've killed him dead!" a man yelled at Mike.

Mike stared, and then he ran over to Carpenter. He bent down, silent.

"It was an accident," Mike said at last. He ran back and picked up Bang-All. He broke the rifle over his knee. He roared with grief. He swore at the bullet and the powder horn, and at the mountains and himself. "It was an accident!" he cried. "I aimed for the cup."

A trapper jeered, "I guess you must be getting old, Mike Fink. I guess maybe you're not the best sharpshooter around!"

Mike turned red in the face, but he didn't say anything.

Another trapper called out, "Hey, Mike, I thought you never missed a shot yet. Just big talk, huh?"

Mike turned purple.

Talbot stepped forward. His eyes were both sharp and sad. "What made you miss, Mike?"

Mike felt a shrill "Whoop!" gather in his throat, as it had every time before when he knew he could out-shoot any man east or west.

"I didn't miss!" he roared at Talbot. "I aimed right for Carpenter's forehead. I'm the greatest sharpshooter that ever drew a bead . . ."

He never finished, because Talbot lifted his own rifle and shot Mike through the heart, not spilling a drop of blood.

Mike slumped to the ground. He had only enough breath left to puff his chest up one final time.

"Whoop!" he roared. "Cock-a-doodle-do! I'm the original Pittsburgh screamer, roarer, and thunderer! I can out-shoot, out-fight, and out-yell anybody anywhere at any time!" He took a final, small breath, and the words came out so faintly that it was almost a whisper. "And I was the best keelboatman that ever lived."

Mike was bragging still, there at the end. But those last words, as everybody knows, were the honest truth.

Davy Crockett

Frontier Fighter

The state of Tennessee wasn't born too many years before Davy Crockett was. In a way, Tennessee and Davy grew up together, and they both grew fast. Davy never became quite as tall as the Great Smoky Mountains, but by the time he was eight years old, he had a good start. All the Crockett family were on the large side. They had to be. Clearing out the wilderness by the Nolachucky River, where Davy first saw the sunrise, took grit and gumption. Davy had plenty of that, and more.

When people wanted to push posts down into the Nola-

chucky's bed to make supports for a bridge, they called Davy
to jump on the posts. Davy would leap from one post to another, pushing them down with his bare feet. He had to be
careful not to jump on a single post more than once or it might
disappear into the river bottom.

He was a handy boy with an axe, too. There was wonderful
timber in Tennessee. Many of the trees were so thick that the
settlers couldn't cut them down, but had to tie chains around
them and let the trees choke themselves to death. Davy could
chop down the biggest sycamores or gum trees with the dull
side of his axe blade.

As for hunting, Davy was the terror of the forest. The wild
animals who were smart would crawl off and hide in their holes,
pulling in their shadows after them, when they saw Davy
coming with his rifle. At other times, when Davy wasn't hunting, the animals liked to spend the time of day with him and
even talk a little. Davy always did know how to talk to animals.

One of the most special things about Davy was his grin. He
could grin from ear to ear, and since his ears were rather far
apart, this made for a sizable grin. He inherited his grin from
his father, who, it was said, could grin in the teeth of a blizzard
and change it into a rainbow. Davy didn't know how powerful
his own grin was, until one day he grinned at a raccoon sitting
in a tree. The raccoon tumbled to the ground, dead right down
to its striped tail.

From then on, Davy did most of his raccoon hunting that
way. One night, he was out hunting with his hound dog Rattler.
It was a clear, crisp night, with the moon spangling the trees and
the wild pea vines, and the frogs croaking in a way that sounded
like *Cr-r-r-ock-k-k-ket*. Davy stood admiring the scenery, slapping at a mosquito or two, when he saw a raccoon sitting high

up in a big tulip tree. It seemed to be a sleek, shining raccoon, though the black mask across its eyes didn't look as dark as usual. Rattler, who generally bellowed when he saw game, didn't even bark.

Davy grinned up at the creature. He grinned for several minutes, but the raccoon stayed where it was.

"Maybe he can't see me clearly enough," Davy said to Rattler, who had gone to sleep. Davy moved where the moonlight was brighter. He set himself to grinning again, looking straight up at the raccoon. The raccoon didn't even twitch a whisker.

Davy began to get a little mad. Also, his grin-muscles were growing tired.

"You fool raccoon!" Davy yelled and shook his fist. "Don't you know you're supposed to fall dead when I grin at you? Ain't I the yallerest blossom in the forest, and all solid brimstone except for my head and ears? If I have to stand here much longer grinning at you, I'll spoil, unless somebody covers me up with salt."

Davy found a large fallen tree branch. He propped it up and leaned his chin against the top end so that he could rest and grin at the same time. He grinned his hardest, showing all his teeth. His grin was so wide it went past his ears and half-way around to the back of his head. It made no difference to the raccoon.

"Well, sir!" said Davy, mad enough to spit nails, but curious too, about the kind of raccoon that could be so stupid it didn't fall dead when it was supposed to. He went back for his axe. The raccoon was still in the tree when Davy returned. Since the tree was rather large, about ten feet thick, he had to hit it twice with the sharp side of the axe.

The tree crashed down. Davy ran to it. Rattler woke up and

ran beside him. Davy searched, and Rattler sniffed. There was no sign of the raccoon. But there was something on a top branch that *looked* like a sleek, shining raccoon.

Davy stared at it, feeling foolish. He had been wasting his time grinning at a large knot on the tree branch. The knot was as bare of bark as a hound's tooth, for Davy had grinned the bark completely off the knot and off all one side of the tree.

Davy still used his rifle, named Betsy, now and then to keep in practice. Near a gap in the Cumberland Mountains one day, he saw a raccoon perched in a cottonwood. It was a real, live raccoon, but it was so sad-looking that Davy had tears in his eyes as he raised his gun.

The raccoon lifted one paw and said in a mournful voice, "Pardon me, mister, but do you happen to be Davy Crockett?"

"I'm one and the same," said Davy.

"In that case," said the raccoon, "I'm as good as dead already, so you can put your rifle away." The raccoon crawled down from the tree and stood with his head bowed as if he were already at his own funeral.

Davy had never met such a respectful raccoon before. He stooped and patted the animal. "You've got such fine manners, little fellow," said Davy, "I want you to go home and raise up more raccoons like yourself."

The raccoon raced off, then remembered his manners. "Thank you, Mister Crockett," he called.

The time came for Davy to get married; so he did. He found a girl called Polly Finley Thunder Whirlwind, who was just the right-size wife for him, being about half as tall as the Northern Lights and twice as good at dancing. Polly had a good-sized grin, too, and she could laugh the mud chinks out of a log cabin. She laughed so hard dancing with Davy one winter that

the cabin was full of holes. The wind naturally poked all its fingers through the holes until everyone nearly froze. They were all too busy shivering to have time for anything else. Davy brought home a half-bald wolf to lie in front of the coldest blast and do the shivering for the whole family, which by then included several children.

Davy brought home another pet, a big, good-natured bear. Davy had gotten caught in an earthquake crack and couldn't get free. A bear passed by, and Davy hung on to him until the

bear pulled him out of the crack. Davy was so thankful, he hugged the bear. The bear hugged Davy back and almost hugged him to death. Davy named the bear Death-Hug and told him that the next time either of them felt affectionate, it would be safer if they just shook hands.

Death-Hug grew tame enough to let Davy put a saddle on his back and ride him like a horse. They traveled and hunted all over Tennessee together, from Lick Creek to the Shakes Country to the Obion River. When they were through traveling around for the day, they would sit and smoke a pipe together. Death-Hug was as fond of smoking as a fireplace with the damper shut.

Around 1812 the War of 1812 began, and Davy went to fight the English and their allies, the Creek Indians. The leader of the American Army was General Andrew Jackson. Jackson was as full of brimstone and dynamite as Davy, so they got along fine.

Davy and Andy Jackson beat the Indians so badly there wasn't much left except their war paint. Then Davy went down to New Orleans with Jackson and fought the British redcoats until the red coats turned pale gray.

When there wasn't any fighting left to do, Davy went home to his spring planting. With him, he took another pet he had picked up in the southern swamp country, a slithering, good-natured, grinning alligator called Old Mississippi.

Davy never lost his own grin in all that time. It was his grin that made him decide to go into politics. In those days, just like today, the politician with the biggest grin was apt to win. Davy went into the woods and practiced making speeches to his animal friends.

The animals figured life would be safer for them if Davy were elected to the state legislature and had to spend his time making laws instead of hunting. So they cheered and paraded, barking and howling. It sounded to Davy as if they were saying, "VOTE FOR CROCKETT." It sounded that way to his neighbors, too, so they went along with the animals and elected Davy to the Tennessee legislature.

Davy put on his foxskin cap, dusted off his fringed buckskin jacket, and set out for Nashville. He rode Death-Hug part of the way and Old Mississippi the rest. Some of the other politicians snickered when they saw him, but Davy paid no attention. All his life he had lived by his motto—*Be sure you're right, then go ahead.* That's what he did then. The Tennessee settlers liked what he did so well that they finally elected him to Congress and sent him to Washington.

Andrew Jackson was President by then. When he saw Davy, he wrapped his arms around him so hard, Davy felt as if Death-Hug had grabbed him. Davy hugged Andy right back. It seemed they might crush each other to death, but when they both got blue in the face, they let go.

Davy had heard about the wonderful dancing that went on in Washington, and had trained Death-Hug and Old Mississippi to dance. Old Mississippi danced on his tail, and Death-Hug danced on his hind legs. Davy, who was a first-class dancer himself, danced the legs off everyone.

When there wasn't any work to be done in Congress, and no dancing or parades, Davy kept busy at other things. One of his biggest jobs was a certain comet that pulled loose from its hinges and started speeding toward the earth. At first, it was only a yellowish speck far off in the sky, its tail sparkling like the tail of a horse on fire. Every day, however, it grew bigger and brighter, coming closer.

Andy Jackson called Davy aside. "Colonel Crockett," he said, "the government has to do something about that comet. If it hits us, we'll all be blown to smithereens, and then some."

"I'll look into the situation, Mr. President," said Davy.

He straddled Death-Hug and rode him to the top of the tallest mountain, figuring on meeting the comet half-way. He got so close to the comet, he began to sweat from its heat.

The comet came closer and closer, wiggling its flaming tail like a fish on a hook. Davy tried grinning it to death, but the comet grinned right back, its teeth like a thousand torches. Davy tried firing his rifle at it, but the bullets melted and dripped off like red butter.

"Well, sir!" said Davy. He bunched up his muscles and prepared to jump. The comet whooshed past him, all set to smash into every one of the thirty states in the Union. Davy stretched his arm out to its full length and grabbed the comet's tail. The comet hissed and thrashed, shooting sparks up to the Milky Way.

Davy started whirling the comet around his head like a lasso. He whirled until the comet grew dizzy and began to wobble. When the comet was too weak even to hiccough, Davy let go. The comet went flying back up into the sky, growing smaller until it was little bigger than a firefly running out of fuel.

Davy lit up his pipe and gave Death-Hug a puff. Then they started back to Washington for a good night's rest.

Around that time, Davy moved his family to Tennessee's western border. The soil there was richer than a multimillionaire. Davy didn't bother to plant seeds in the regular way; he loaded his shotgun with the seeds and shot them into the ground. Pumpkin vines grew so fast that the pumpkins were worn out from being dragged across the soil. A man had to be a fast runner even to pick one.

Things went along fine, until the time of the Big Freeze. The winter started out cold and grew colder. By January, it was so cold that smoke froze in fireplace chimneys. Davy's hair froze so stiff he didn't dare comb it, for fear it would crack. One morning, daybreak froze solid. When that happened, it became so cold that people didn't even dare think about it, because their thoughts froze right inside their heads.

Davy told his wife Polly, "I reckon I better amble around the country and see what in tarnation the trouble is."

He put on a foxskin cap and several coonskin caps on over it. He piled on a half-dozen jackets and several pairs of bearskin mittens. He put on so many socks that he had to stand on his head between times to rest his feet. When he left, he took a homemade bear trap with him. Davy walked all day, going toward Cloud Mountain. To keep from freezing to death, he had to shinny up and down a tree all night.

In the morning, he saw what the trouble was. The machinery that kept the earth turning had frozen. The gears and wheels couldn't move, and the sun had been caught between two blocks of ice under the wheels. The sun had worked so hard to get loose that it had frozen in its own icy sweat.

Davy set the bear trap and caught an exceptionally fat bear. He took the bear and held him up over the earth's frozen machinery. Then Davy squeezed the bear until slippery, hot bear oil ran down over the wheels and gears. Next, he greased the sun's face until the oil melted the ice.

"Get moving!" Davy ordered and gave one of the wheels a kick with his heel.

There was a creak, which changed to a whir as the earth

began to turn again. The sun rolled over and flipped free. As it circled past, Davy lit his pipe from its trailing sparks. Then he stuck an especially bright piece of sunrise in his pocket and started for home.

On the way, he decided to do a little hunting, since he had a double-barreled shotgun with him. He was just aiming the gun at a flock of wild geese flying near, when he saw a big buck deer. He waited for the geese to come near the buck, figuring he could get both the geese and the deer with one shot. Suddenly, a rattlesnake started rattling its loud tail right at Davy's feet, ready to strike. Davy gave the geese a blast from one barrel of his gun, and the buck a blast from the other. The gun kicked hard against Davy's shoulder and flew out of his hands. It flattened the snake and knocked Davy into a nearby river.

Davy climbed out of the water in such a hurry that his clothes were still dry. His pockets were loaded down with goggle-eyed perch. The weight of the fish pulled at his jacket and made the buttons pop off. One button hit a doe deer, and the other hit a squirrel, and they both died immediately from surprise.

Davy reached home lugging a bundle of geese, a swarm of fish, two deer, a rattlesnake, and a squirrel in his free hand. When he told his neighbors he had killed them all with one shot, one of the settlers said, "You're a clapper-clawing liar, Davy Crockett."

"Oh, I only lie enough to keep myself happy," said Davy, and he pulled out the scrap of sunrise for the children to play with.

Most of the people were grateful to Davy for breaking the cold snap, but some began saying Davy wasted his time in Congress dancing, parading, and telling tall tales. When voting time came again, enough people voted against Davy for him to lose the election.

"Well, sir!" said Davy, feeling as hot around his collar as he had when he had fought the comet. "From now on, the people of Tennessee will get no help from me! Anyhow, the state's getting too crowded. I'm moving to Texas!"

When the Texas animals heard that Davy Crockett was coming, half of them fled across the border to Mexico. About a third of the buffalo—the meanest and toughest—remained. Buffalo didn't scare Davy, even the orneriest of them. One day, he caught two of the biggest buffalo bulls in Texas and tied their tails together in a bow knot. Davy made a personal pet of one of the bulls and took the creature to church with him. This buffalo had such a fine bass voice, he was the best singer in the church choir.

Texas in those days was a part of Mexico. Davy and many of the other American settlers didn't like taking orders from the Mexican government. So Davy and his friends decided to make their own laws. When Santa Anna, the President of Mexico, heard this, he ordered his army to go northward and beat the tar out of the rebel Americans.

According to some people, Davy killed enough buffalo to feed the whole Texas army. He roasted the meat by racing along behind the flames of a prairie fire. Also, they say, he talked so many of the animals over to the American side, including wildcats, snakes, wolves, and mountain lions, that he scared the Mexican soldiers out of their boots.

The people who write history books say that Davy died fighting the Mexicans in San Antonio, Texas, at a fort called the Alamo. No one has ever said whether Death-Hug and Old Mississippi were with him. The chances are that they were and fought beside him to the end, since they have never been seen since.

One thing is certain. The sun comes up in Texas and in Tennessee every day, summer or winter. And the earth keeps turning smoothly, the way it's supposed to. If it ever does get frozen fast again, Davy Crockett may come along to squeeze some bear oil over the works and give the wheels a kick to start everything humming once more.

Johnny Appleseed

Rainbow-walker

No one has ever counted all the apple trees in America, but there are a lot of them. According to some people, we have all these apple orchards because a man called Johnny Appleseed (his real name was John Chapman) spent his life planting apple seeds. That was back in the days when most of our country was still a wilderness.

Johnny Appleseed loved apple trees more than almost anything else. He loved animals, too; some say he could talk to them. When he was still a small boy in Boston, people brought hurt or sick animals to him. Johnny had a kind of magic in his hands that helped him to heal hurt creatures, just as it helped him to grow trees and plants.

One day, when Johnny was a young man, a stranger came by Johnny's house. Johnny was picking apples from the ground, where the wind had blown them.

The man stopped and said, "I haven't seen apples like that in two years."

"Where have you been?" Johnny asked him.

"Working on a flatboat out west in the Indian country. There aren't any apple trees growing out there. I'd like to buy a sack of your apples. Maybe they'll keep long enough for my wife and children back in the Ohio Territory to enjoy them."

Johnny fixed up a sackful. "I don't want any money," he said. "Just save the seeds when you get home, and plant them."

"That's a good idea, young fellow," the man said. "Thanks."

Johnny sat down under one of the apple trees and thought about what the man had said. Many families were moving west. If they carried apple seeds with them and planted them, there would be orchards sprouting up all over. Johnny knew his own orchard wasn't large enough to provide all the seeds needed. And there weren't as many settlers starting out from Boston as from a place like Pittsburgh, which was farther west.

Johnny thought a long time. Then he began gathering all the apple seeds from the apples on the ground. Before long, he had a small leather sack full of seeds.

A house sparrow flew down to pick up one of the seeds which had fallen from the sack.

"You leave that seed be, Mrs. Sparrow," Johnny said. "That's going to be an apple tree."

Two small boys going by heard him. "There's that loony Johnny, talking to himself again," one said.

"My folks say he's light in the head," the other said.

Johnny heard them and laughed, rolling a firm, red apple in his hands. He did not care what people said.

The next day, Johnny put the sackful of seeds over his shoulder and a small bundle of food in his pocket and started walking toward Pittsburgh. The dust spurted up in small clouds behind his bare heels. The wind made his long, black hair stand out behind his ears. Off in the distance, in the direction he was going, a rainbow shone in the sky, pink and yellow, green and blue. To Johnny the pink was the color of apple blossoms, and the pale green was the color of apples before they were ripe.

It took Johnny quite a long while to reach Pittsburgh. When he got there, he worked until he had enough money to buy a piece of ground. Then he started planting an apple orchard. Before long, apple trees were sprouting up around him like grass. As soon as the trees were large enough to bear fruit, Johnny gathered the seeds.

Whenever the people traveling west stopped to ask Johnny for food or water or a place to rest, he gave them apple seeds as well. And he never took any money.

"That's no way to run a business," some of the travelers said.

Johnny laughed. "I like giving orchards away."

People said, "That Johnny Appleseed is crazy."

Johnny kept on giving away sackfuls of seeds. He gave them to farmers and hunters, trappers and boatmen, soldiers and settlers. One day, he realized that he would have to find more seeds than his orchard could produce. He knew that all around Pennsylvania in the fall people put apples into wooden presses.

They squashed and squeezed the apples to get out the bubbling juice for apple cider. And they threw the bright brown seeds away.

"I'm going to go out and get all those wasted seeds," Johnny said to a squirrel he had tamed.

The squirrel waved its tail and said, "Ch-kk, ch-kk," which to Johnny sounded like, "Go ahead."

Johnny put on his hat. It was a strange hat, for it was a kettle turned upside down. But it was more than a hat. It was something handy to cook in, if he stopped by the side of the road and wanted hot food. He looked around for some good traveling clothes. Everything he had was in rags. He saw a pile of gunny sacks which he used for gathering apples. He picked out the longest sack, cut holes in it for his head and arms, and put it on. Nobody could want a better traveling suit, thought Johnny.

Johnny Appleseed went walking up and down and back and forth across Pennsylvania. The Dutch farmers let him have the apple mash from their cider presses. Then, all winter long, Johnny picked out the seeds and dried them. In the spring, he gave the seeds away to anyone who stopped on his way west.

Sometimes, when settlers came back from the western territories, Johnny would ask, "Did you plant the seeds I gave you?"

Often, a settler would answer, "Oh, I forgot."

So, Johnny decided to go west himself and plant his own orchards. He rigged up a boat by lashing two canoes together, loaded them full of apple seeds, and set off down the Ohio River.

That was the only time Johnny used a boat. From then on he walked, hundreds and thousands of miles, carrying apple seeds with him. Most of the time he went barefoot, tramping through rain and snow. Wherever settlers gave him a small piece of land, he planted his orchards. Soon there were apple trees grow-ing along the creeks and rivers all over Ohio and Indiana.

It was hard work, but Johnny did not think of it as work. It was what he wanted to do. Every time a sapling burst into bloom, he forgot about his tired feet and the iron kettle hat bumping his forehead. He slept out in the open most of the time, with only the sky for a cover and a fox or raccoon curled up beside him to help keep him warm. When it snowed or rained, he slept in a settler's barn. And sometimes he stayed with Indians.

Johnny had many Indian friends, even though most Indians in those days hated the white men, who were taking over their land.

"Johnny Appleseed is crazy," some of the white men said.

"He is a powerful medicine man," most of the Indians said. "He heals the sick babies and warriors. He makes good medicine from the plants, and he talks to the animals."

Often, Johnny walked through areas where there were neither kindly settlers nor Indians. One bitterly cold night, the only shelter he could find was a large, hollow log. Johnny crawled into the log. He had gone only a few feet when he bumped into something big and soft, and he heard a sleepy, growling noise. It was dark inside the log, but Johnny could make out two eyes looking at him. The eyes belonged to a bear who had decided the log would make a fine bedroom for his winter's sleep.

Johnny calmly said, "Excuse me, Brother Bear," and crawled back out.

On another time, in the late summer, Johnny was resting at the end of the day. He had built a fire to heat up some cornmeal mush in his kettle hat. Suddenly, Johnny noticed that the air was full of flying sparks. The sparks headed toward the fire instead of shooting up from it as actual sparks would do. He looked closer and saw the sparks were tiny, buzzing insects. The insects were blinded by the flames and flew into the fire, where they burned.

Johnny jumped up and put out his fire, even though the cornmeal had not yet cooked. It was better to eat cold food, thought Johnny, than to have any living thing die because of his fire.

There are many tales about Johnny's traveling through the forests without any fear of wild animals. One of the stories people tell is about Johnny and a wolf.

One day, Johnny was busy gathering certain plants, called herbs, which were useful in curing sick people and animals. He was picking some wild ginger, when he heard a long, whimpering howl.

Johnny turned and saw a large black wolf. The wolf saw Johnny, too, and snarled, but it did not move. Johnny walked toward the animal, saying, "I am a friend, Brother Wolf."

The wolf snarled again, and then Johnny saw that its foot was caught in a steel trap.

"Poor beast," Johnny said. He bent down and worked open the jaws of the trap. "Now you are free," he told the wolf.

The wolf hopped back a step and then fell. The leg which had been caught in the trap was bleeding.

Johnny reached out and stroked the wolf's dark, sharp ears. The wolf showed its teeth.

"Don't be afraid," Johnny said. He took a pack from his shoulders, drew out some cloth strips, and bandaged the wolf's leg. When he was through, the wolf licked Johnny's wrist.

It took several days for the wolf's leg to heal. Johnny Appleseed stayed with the animal and took care of it. He fed the wolf and brought it water in his metal hat. When the wolf was well,

Johnny started off on his travels again, his seed packs swinging in time with his step.

He had walked only about a hundred feet when he heard something padding along behind him. It was the black wolf.

From then on, wherever Johnny went, the wolf followed. At night, they slept together under the stars, or huddled in a cave together, out of the rain. By day, they went from cabin to cabin, and some say the great wolf would dig holes with his paws for Johnny's apple seeds.

Johnny began to carry other things besides seeds. He put small gifts into the bags swinging from his shoulders—dolls he had whittled out of wood, pieces of bright cloth or ribbons, pretty speckled stones he had found, or berries to put on a string for a necklace. He gave most of these things to the settlers' children.

Johnny's eyes stayed as bright as ever, even though his dark hair began to turn gray. The black wolf that traveled with him grew old like Johnny, and the wolf's eyes grew dim. The wolf trotted close at Johnny's heels, for that was the only way it could keep on the path. People say that because Johnny loved all wild creatures so much, the wolf learned to love them too. Rabbits would come and drink from the same pool where the wolf drank. Birds would ride on Brother Wolf's shoulder. Even the settlers, who distrusted wolves, learned to like Johnny's wolf.

But one night, a farmer who was new to the frontier saw the huge wolf near his chicken yard. The farmer put his shotgun against his shoulder and aimed.

Johnny Appleseed cried out to stop the farmer, but it was too late. The gun thundered, and the pet wolf leaped into the air as the shot hit its heart. The wolf fell back to earth and lay still.

Johnny sat for a long while beside his dead companion,

stroking the thick fur. He looked up into the sky, seeking some brightness to drive away the gray sorrow he felt. But the sky was clouded over, without stars.

Johnny dug a grave for Brother Wolf by the side of a creek. After he had covered his old, faithful friend with soft earth, he reached into his pouch of apple seeds. He found the brightest, smoothest seeds of all, and carefully planted them around the grave.

Today, people say the spot is filled with apple trees with trunks as big as the legs of elephants. And they say that in spring the blossoms are so thick, a bee can scarcely fly between them.

After the wolf died, Johnny went on alone, still giving away apple seeds, and still planting orchards. The owls followed him at night, and even the shy deer would come out to meet him on the woodland trails at morning. But none stayed with him night and day, as the gentle black wolf had done.

Even though he felt lonely, Johnny was happy. Wherever he stopped, he handed out his seeds and preached about the beauty of things. He also preached about the need for kindness, especially kindness to animals. When settlers had horses too old to work any more, or too lame to be of use, they sometimes turned these horses out into the woods to die. When Johnny came across these animals, he took care of them and found them new homes.

He went on and on in his ragged clothes and his clanging hat, planting trees. Everywhere he went orchards sprang up. Where only weeds or brush had been, there was cloud on cloud of apple blossoms.

"He's loony, that Johnny Appleseed," some people said.

"He's lightheaded, that's certain," others agreed.

Johnny laughed, for he did not care what people said. He walked on, his bare heels kicking the leaves aside, until one day he was too tired to walk any farther.

On that day, he crawled into a small orchard near Fort Wayne, Indiana. He put one of his seed pouches under his head for a pillow. He lay there, looking up at the waving branches of apple trees and at the blue sky shining beyond.

Johnny Appleseed closed his eyes, listening to the leaves clapping together overhead. The sound faded, and the world turned dark. Then, suddenly, Johnny heard a soft whining. He thought he saw Brother Wolf standing beside him, his pink tongue hanging out as if he had traveled a long, long way. And there, hopping about among the tree roots, was Mrs. Sparrow. There, too, was the big, sleepy bear Johnny had met years before in the round darkness of a hollow log. And creeping out of the orchard shadows came raccoons and foxes, bobolinks and hummingbirds, shy deer, and lame, blinking horses.

Johnny sat up, rubbing his eyes. He looked at the sky again. Shimmering in the air, like a bridge of braided flowers, was a rainbow.

Johnny Appleseed leaped to his feet. He picked up all of his seed pouches and slung them over his shoulder. Then he called to the animals, "Brother Wolf, Sister Sparrow, Brother Bear . . ."

He started up the rainbow. The animals and the birds followed. Brother Wolf was the first, tagging at Johnny Appleseed's heels. Two orioles rode on the wolf's shoulders.

When they all reached the top of the rainbow, Johnny began throwing apple seeds all over the sky. If they stuck in the sky, they would grow into stars. If they fell to earth, they would become trees. Johnny looked down at the land covered with orchards and knew his work was done.

The next morning, a traveler going westward paused by the apple orchard where Johnny had stopped to rest. Under the brightest tree of all lay the small body of Johnny Appleseed, still dressed in a gunny sack and still wearing his strange kettle hat. All around him, sitting in a quiet circle, were wild animals.

The traveler started on his way, planning to tell the nearest settler of what he had found. Then he saw three bright brown apple seeds lying at his feet. He picked them up and took them with him, wondering where he should plant them.

That is what some people say. Judging by all the apple trees there are, east and west, north and south, it seems someone must have carried on the planting Johnny Appleseed began.

John Henry

Hammerman

People down South still tell stories about John Henry, how strong he was, and how he could whirl a big sledge so lightning-fast you could hear thunder behind it. They even say he was born with a hammer in his hand. John Henry himself said it, but he probably didn't mean it exactly as it sounded.

The story seems to be that when John Henry was a baby, the first thing he reached out for was a hammer which was hung nearby on the cabin wall.

John Henry's father put his arm around his wife's shoulder.

"He's going to grow up to be a steel-driving man. I can see it plain as rows of cotton running uphill."

As John Henry grew a bit older, he practiced swinging the hammer, not hitting at things, but just enjoying the feel of it whooshing against the air. When he was old enough to talk, he told everyone, "I was born with a hammer in my hand."

John Henry was still a boy when the Civil War started, but he was a big, hard-muscled boy, and he could out-work and out-play all the other Negro boys on the plantation.

"You're going to be a mighty man, John Henry," his father told him.

"A man ain't nothing but a man," young John Henry said. "And I'm a natural man, born to swing a hammer in my hand."

At night, lying on a straw bed on the floor, John Henry listened to a far-off train whistling through the darkness. Railroad tracks had been laid to carry trainloads of Southern soldiers to fight against the armies of the North. The trains had a lonesome, longing sound that made John Henry want to go wherever they were going.

When the war ended, a man from the North came to John Henry where he was working in the field. He said, "The slaves are free now. You can pack up and go wherever you want, young fellow."

"I'm craving to go where the trains go," said John Henry.

The man shook his head. "There are too many young fellows trailing the trains around now. You better settle down to doing what you know, like handling a cotton hook or driving a mule team."

John Henry thought to himself, there's a big hammer waiting for me somewhere, because I know I'm a steel-driving man. All I have to do is hunt 'til I find it.

That night, he told his folks about a dream he had had.

"I dreamed I was working on a railroad somewhere," he said, "a big, new railroad called the C. & O., and I had a mighty hammer in my hand. Every time I swung it, it made a whirling flash around my shoulder. And every time my hammer hit a spike, the sky lit up from the sparks."

"I believe it," his father said. "You were born to drive steel."

"That ain't all of the dream," John Henry said. "I dreamed that the railroad was going to be the end of me and I'd die with the hammer in my hand."

The next morning, John Henry bundled up some food in a red bandanna handkerchief, told his parents good-by, and set off into the world. He walked until he heard the clang-clang of hammers in the distance. He followed the sound to a place where gangs of men were building a railroad. John Henry watched the men driving steel spikes down into the crossties to hold the rails in place. Three men would stand around a spike, then each, in turn, would swing a long hammer.

John Henry's heart beat in rhythm with the falling hammers. His fingers ached for the feel of a hammer in his own hands. He walked over to the foreman.

"I'm a natural steel-driving man," he said. "And I'm looking for a job."

"How much steel-driving have you done?" the foreman asked.

"I was born knowing how," John Henry said.

The foreman shook his head. "That ain't good enough, boy. I can't take any chances. Steel-driving's dangerous work, and you might hit somebody."

"I wouldn't hit anybody," John Henry said, "because I can drive one of those spikes all by myself."

The foreman said sharply, "The one kind of man I don't need in this outfit is a bragger. Stop wasting my time."

John Henry didn't move. He got a stubborn look around his jaw. "You loan me a hammer, boss mister, and if somebody will hold the spike for me, I'll prove what I can do."

The three men who had just finished driving in a spike looked toward him and laughed. One of them said, "Anybody who would hold a spike for a greenhorn don't want to live long."

"I'll hold it," a fourth man said.

John Henry saw that the speaker was a small, dark-skinned fellow about his own age.

The foreman asked the small man, "D'you aim to get yourself killed, Li'l Willie?"

Li'l Willie didn't answer. He knelt and set a spike down through the rail on the crosstie. "Come on, big boy," he said.

John Henry picked up one of the sheep-nose hammers lying in the cinders. He hefted it and decided it was too light. He picked up a larger one which weighed twelve pounds. The handle was lean and limber and greased with tallow to make it smooth.

Everyone was quiet, watching, as he stepped over to the spike.

John Henry swung the hammer over his shoulder so far that the hammer head hung down against the back of his knees. He felt a thrill run through his arms and chest.

"Tap it down gentle, first," said Li'l Willie.

But John Henry had already started to swing. He brought the hammer flashing down, banging the spike squarely on the head. Before the other men could draw a breath of surprise, the hammer flashed again, whirring through the air like a giant hummingbird. One more swing, and the spike was down, its steel head smoking from the force of the blow.

The foreman blinked, swallowed, and blinked again. "Man," he told John Henry, "you're hired!"

That's the way John Henry started steel-driving. From then on, Li'l Willie was always with him, setting the spikes, or placing the drills that John Henry drove with his hammer. There wasn't another steel-driving man in the world who could touch John Henry for speed and power. He could hammer every which way, up or down or sidewise. He could drive for ten hours at a stretch and never miss a stroke.

After he'd been at the work for a few years, he started using a twenty-pound hammer in each hand. It took six men, working fast, to carry fresh drills to him. People would come for miles around to watch John Henry.

Whenever John Henry worked, he sang. Li'l Willie sang with him, chanting the rhythm of the clanging hammer strokes.

Those were happy days for John Henry. One of the happiest days came when he met a black-eyed, curly-haired girl called Polly Ann. And, on the day that Polly Ann said she would marry him, John Henry almost burst his throat with singing.

Every now and then, John Henry would remember the strange dream he had had years before, about the C. & O. Railroad and dying with a hammer in his hand. One night, he had the dream again. The next morning, when he went to work, the steel gang gathered round him, hopping with excitement.

"The Chesapeake and Ohio Railroad wants men to drive a tunnel through a mountain in West Virginia!" they said.

"The C. & O. wants the best hammermen there are!" they said. "And they'll pay twice as much as anybody else."

Li'l Willie looked at John Henry. "If they want the best, John Henry, they're goin' to need you."

John Henry looked back at his friend. "They're going to need

92

you, too, Li'l Willie. I ain't going without you." He stood a minute, looking at the sky. There was a black thundercloud way off, with sunlight flashing behind it. John Henry felt a small chill between his shoulder blades. He shook himself, put his hammer on his shoulder, and said, "Let's go, Willie!"

When they reached Summers County where the Big Bend Tunnel was to be built, John Henry sized up the mountain standing in the way. It was almost solid rock.

"Looks soft," said John Henry. "Hold a drill up there, Li'l Willie."

Li'l Willie did. John Henry took a seventy-pound hammer and drove the drill in with one mountain-cracking stroke. Then he settled down to working the regular way, pounding in the drills with four or five strokes of a twenty-pound sledge. He worked so fast that his helpers had to keep buckets of water ready to pour on his hammers so they wouldn't catch fire.

Polly Ann, who had come along to West Virginia, sat and watched and cheered him on. She sang along with him, clapping her hands to the rhythm of his hammer, and the sound echoed around the mountains. The songs blended with the rumble of dynamite where the blasting crews were at work. For every time John Henry drilled a hole in the mountain's face, other men poked dynamite and black powder into the hole and then lighted a fuse to blow the rock apart.

One day the tunnel boss Cap'n Tommy Walters was standing watching John Henry, when a stranger in city clothes walked up to him.

"Howdy, Cap'n Tommy," said the stranger. "I'd like to talk to you about a steam engine I've got for sale. My engine can drive a drill through rock so fast that not even a crew of your best men can keep up with it."

"I don't need any machine," Cap'n Tommy said proudly. "My man John Henry can out-drill any machine ever built."

"I'll place a bet with you, Cap'n," said the salesman. "You race your man against my machine for a full day. If he wins, I'll give you the steam engine free."

Cap'n Tommy thought it over. "That sounds fair enough, but I'll have to talk to John Henry first." He told John Henry what the stranger had said. "Are you willing to race a steam drill?" Cap'n Tommy asked.

John Henry ran his big hands over the handle of his hammer, feeling the strength in the wood and in his own great muscles.

"A man's a man," he said, "but a machine ain't nothing but a machine. I'll beat that steam drill, or I'll die with my hammer in my hand!"

"All right, then," said Cap'n Tommy. "We'll set a day for the contest."

Polly Ann looked worried when John Henry told her what he had promised to do.

"Don't you worry, honey," John Henry said. It was the end of the workday, with the sunset burning across the mountain, and the sky shining like copper. He tapped his chest. "I've got a man's heart in here. All a machine has is a metal engine." He smiled and picked Polly Ann up in his arms, as if she were no heavier than a blade of grass.

On the morning of the contest, the slopes around the tunnel were crowded with people. At one side stood the steam engine, its gears and valves and mechanical drill gleaming. Its operators rushed around, giving it final spurts of grease and oil and shoving fresh pine knots into the fire that fed the steam boiler.

John Henry stood leaning on his hammer, as still as the

mountain rock, his shoulders shining like hard coal in the rising sun.

"How do you feel, John Henry?" asked Li'l Willie. Li'l Willie's hands trembled a bit as he held the drill ready.

"I feel like a bird ready to bust out of a nest egg," John Henry said. "I feel like a rooster ready to crow. I feel pride hammering at my heart, and I can hardly wait to get started against that machine." He sucked in the mountain air. "I feel powerful free, Li'l Willie."

Cap'n Tommy held up the starting gun. For a second everything was as silent as the dust in a drill hole. Then the gun barked, making a yelp that bounced against mountain and sky.

John Henry swung his hammer, and it rang against the drill.

At the same time, the steam engine gave a roar and a hiss. Steam whistled through its escape valve. Its drill crashed down, gnawing into the granite.

John Henry paid no attention to anything except his hammer, nor to any sound except the steady pumping of his heart. At the end of an hour, he paused long enough to ask, "How are we doing, Li'l Willie?"

Willie licked his lips. His face was pale with rock dust and with fear. "The machine's ahead, John Henry."

John Henry tossed his smoking hammer aside and called to another helper, "Bring me two hammers! I'm only getting warmed up."

He began swinging a hammer in each hand. Sparks flew so fast and hot they singed his face. The hammers heated up until they glowed like torches.

"How're we doing now, Li'l Willie?" John Henry asked at the end of another hour.

Li'l Willie grinned. "The machine's drill busted. They have to take time to fix up a new one. You're almost even now, John Henry! How're you feeling?"

"I'm feeling like sunrise," John Henry took time to say before he flashed one of his hammers down against the drill. "Clean out the hole, Willie, and we'll drive right down to China."

Above the clash of his hammers, he heard the chug and hiss of the steam engine starting up again and the whine of its rotary drill biting into rock. The sound hurt John Henry's ears.

"Sing me a song, Li'l Willie!" he gasped. "Sing me a natural song for my hammers to sing along with."

Li'l Willie sang, and John Henry kept his hammers going in time. Hour after hour, he kept driving, sweat sliding from his forehead and chest.

The sun rolled past noon and toward the west.

"How're you feeling, John Henry?" Li'l Willie asked.

"I ain't tired yet," said John Henry and stood back, gasping, while Willie put a freshly sharpened drill into the rock wall. "Only, I have a kind of roaring in my ears."

"That's only the steam engine," Li'l Willie said, but he wet his lips again. "You're gaining on it, John Henry. I reckon you're at least two inches ahead."

John Henry coughed and slung his hammer back. "I'll beat it by a mile, before the sun sets."

At the end of another hour, Li'l Willie called out, his eyes sparkling, "You're going to win, John Henry, if you can keep on drivin'!"

John Henry ground his teeth together and tried not to hear the roar in his ears or the racing thunder of his heart. "I'll go until I drop," he gasped. "I'm a steel-driving man and I'm bound to win, because a machine ain't nothing but a machine."

The sun slid lower. The shadows of the crowd grew long and purple.

"John Henry can't keep it up," someone said.

"The machine can't keep it up," another said.

Polly Ann twisted her hands together and waited for Cap'n Tommy to fire the gun to mark the end of the contest.

"Who's winning?" a voice cried.

"Wait and see," another voice answered.

There were only ten minutes left.

"How're you feeling, John Henry?" Li'l Willie whispered, sweat dripping down his own face.

John Henry didn't answer. He just kept slamming his hammers against the drill, his mouth open.

Li'l Willie tried to go on singing. "Flash that hammer—uh! Wham that drill—uh!" he croaked.

Out beside the railroad tracks, Polly beat her hands together in time, until they were numb.

The sun flared an instant, then died behind the mountain. Cap'n Tommy's gun cracked. The judges ran forward to measure the depth of the holes drilled by the steam engine and by John Henry. At last, the judges came walking back and said something to Cap'n Tommy before they turned to announce their findings to the crowd.

Cap'n Tommy walked over to John Henry, who stood leaning against the face of the mountain.

"John Henry," he said, "you beat that steam engine by four feet!" He held out his hand and smiled.

John Henry heard a distant cheering. He held his own hand out, and then he staggered. He fell and lay on his back, staring up at the mountain and the sky, and then he saw Polly Ann and Li'l Willie leaning over him.

"Oh, how do you feel, John Henry?" Polly Ann asked.

"I feel a bit tuckered out," said John Henry.

"Do you want me to sing to you?" Li'l Willie asked.

"I got a song in my own heart, thank you, Li'l Willie," John Henry said. He raised up on his elbow and looked at all the people and the last sunset light gleaming like the edge of a golden trumpet. "I was a steel-driving man," he said, and lay back and closed his eyes forever.

Down South, and in the North, too, people still talk about

John Henry and how he beat the steam engine at the Big Bend Tunnel. They say, if John Henry were alive today, he could beat almost every other kind of machine, too.

Maybe so. At least, John Henry would die trying.

Joe Magarac

Steelmaker

Often, when the furnaces of the steel mills around Pittsburgh are going full blast, turning the sky a deep red with their fire, people say, "Joe Magarac must be back on the job."

It was a long time ago that Joe Magarac appeared among the Hungarian steelworkers in the part of Pittsburgh called Hunkietown. No one is certain where he came from. Some say he came right out of the rolling mills with the steel. Others say he came out of a huge ore pit. The first anyone saw of him was at a party in Hunkietown.

The party was put on by a steelworker called Steve Mestrovich, and it was no ordinary party. Big Steve sent invitations to everyone in the steel mill towns up and down the valley.

"My daughter is ready to marry," Big Steve said. "She is the most beautiful girl in Allegheny County. She must have a very strong man for her husband. So, I am holding a contest to find who is strongest, and then we'll have a big wedding."

On the day of the event, lines of people came from all the nearby towns. They came chattering and singing, riding in river boats, driving teams of horses, or walking. The women wore their brightest scarves, and the men wore their fanciest jackets. The young men twirled their mustaches and boasted how they would win Mary Mestrovich.

Everyone gathered around the platform and tables Big Steve had set up in a field above the river. The young men bragged and flexed their muscles while they drank prune jack and ate Hungarian meat soup and cheese noodles. They kept looking toward the platform where Mary sat in a red and green silk dress, her yellow hair shining under a red scarf.

"I'm the best man for Mary," said Pete Pussick from Hunkietown. He tapped his chest and smiled at Mary. Mary smiled back.

"You talk like a boaster," said Eli Stanoski, another Hunkietown man. "I'm the best." He smiled at Mary, but she paid no attention.

A stranger from Johnstown, with muscles as big as barrels, swaggered over to the platform and offered Mary some rock candy. Mary kept on smiling at Pete Pussick.

Steve Mestrovich stood up finally and said it was time for the contest to start. "I have iron bars brought here from the mill," he told the crowd. "The first bar is for little, weak fellows—it weighs only three hundred and fifty pounds. The second bar weighs five hundred. The third will make somebody sweat, maybe, for it weighs as much as the other two together."

Pete Pussick and the rest pulled off their shirts and stepped over to the iron bars lying on the ground near Mary's platform.

Pete smiled at Mary, and she smiled back at him. Then he leaned down and lifted the first bar without a grunt. Eli Stanoski was next. He raised the bar as easily as Pete had. Two steel workers from Homestead tried next, and failed, but the big man from Johnstown hoisted the bar with a shrug.

"I'm the best man for you," Pete whispered to Mary. She handed him a geranium blossom that she wore in her hair.

Pete stepped over to the second, heavier bar. He set his muscles, gritted his teeth, and lifted the iron. Eli, also, managed to lift the second bar. The rest grunted and sweated and struggled, but the only other one who could raise the bar from the ground was the big man from Johnstown.

Big Steve and the rest of the Hunkietown people were worried. They did not like the idea of a stranger winning Mary and taking her off to Johnstown to live. Anyhow, they knew that Mary wanted Pete Pussick to be the winner.

Everyone was silent as Pete bent over the third bar. He spit on his hands and spread his feet wide. He stooped down and grabbed the bar. He pulled and strained until his face was as red as if he were working in front of an open-hearth furnace. Pete could not move the bar an inch off the ground. He gave up and stood with his head down, not looking at Mary.

Eli took his turn. He pulled and panted and groaned, but the bar did not budge.

The Johnstown man stroked the ends of his big mustache and walked up to the bar. He looked at it as if it were only a broom handle lying there. He planted his feet wide, bent over, and took hold of it. He gave a big pull but nothing happened. He tried again, pulling so hard that it seemed both his hands would fall off. The bar did not move.

Suddenly, there was a booming laugh from somewhere in the crowd: "Ho! Ho! Ho!"

The man from Johnstown turned around, his face redder than the sparks from a shower of red-hot metal. "Who's that laughing at me? If somebody here thinks he's so strong, let him pick up this bar! I'll lift him up and break him in two!"

A big, black-haired man walked forward from the crowd. No one had noticed him before, because everyone was watching the contest. His back was as broad as an ore car, and his wrists were as big around as Mary's waist. He was munching on two roasted paprika chickens and was laughing between bites.

The Johnstown man hitched up his trousers and balled his hands into fists. "I'll teach you to laugh at me!" he shouted.

The big man laughed again. He picked the Johnstown man up in one hand and the iron bar up in the other and shook them both so hard that the Johnstown man's teeth rattled.

Big Steve ran forward. "Hey you, big man—are you trying to kill him?"

The stranger set the Johnstown man down gently. "I don't want to hurt him. I'm just having a little fun." He twisted the iron bar into a figure-eight and tossed it aside.

Big Steve gulped. "What kind of man are you?" he asked. "What is your name?"

"Me, I'm Joe Magarac," the stranger said.

Everyone laughed and put their hands up against their heads, wiggling them like long ears. For the word *magarac* in Hungarian means jackass.

"Joe Jackass," the Johnstown fellow said, snickering at a safe distance.

"Sure, that's me," Joe Magarac said, laughing right along with everyone else. "All I do is eat and work, like a jackass donkey. I came here out of the ore pit to be the best steelman in the whole world. I tell you the truth. Look, I'll show you something!" He pulled off his shirt.

Everyone stared, and then they shielded their eyes, because the sunlight hitting Joe Magarac's chest made it glitter like polished steel.

"Tap your fist there, man," Joe Magarac said, looking around.

Only Big Steve had the courage to rap his knuckles against Joe's chest. There was a sound like ringing metal, and a spark, as Steve's ring scraped across Joe's ribs.

Steve shook his head in disbelief. "He's not telling a lie," he said. "He's a steelman, all right. He's steel from head to foot. And he's the strongest man I've ever seen." He turned and walked over to the platform where Mary sat, and held his hand up to her. "I've found you a big, strong husband, so now we'll have a wedding."

Mary looked at Joe Magarac, and then she looked at Pete Pussick. Her eyes were as blue as the cornflowers back in Hungary, but now they looked a rainy blue because of the tears suddenly glistening there. Her lips, which were usually as red as Hungarian poppies, looked pale. Everyone could see she did not want to marry a man of steel. But she followed her father silently to where Joe Magarac stood.

Joe Magarac looked at her a long time. "You're a pretty girl," he said at last. "You'll be a fine wife for somebody. But me, I only have time to work and to eat. That's my business, not to sit around a house with a wife. I think that young man over there will make you a better husband." He looked toward Pete Pussick. "He's the strongest man here, next to me."

Mary was too happy to speak. Her lips grew red again, and the only tears left in her eyes were tears of happiness.

Big Steve was happy, too. He clapped Joe Magarac on the back and told everyone, "Now we have the wedding, and a big dance afterward. Joe gets first chance to dance with the bride."

"Me, I have no time to dance," laughed Joe Magarac. "Only time to eat and work."

Steve ordered his wife to bring Joe all the meat soup and noodles, paprika chicken, fat, spicy sausages, and brown loaves of bread he could eat. Joe ate right through the wedding ceremony, and he ate for three hours more while the crowd danced to the violins and tambourines. Then he got up, told the Mestroviches good-by, and went off toward the steel mills.

He stopped at a boardinghouse by the mill gate and knocked at the door. A short, plump woman appeared and said, "I'm Mrs. Horkey. Do you want to rent a room?"

"Oh, I don't want a room," Joe Magarac told her. "I want just five big meals each day. The rest of the time I'll be working to turn out steel, day and night." He laughed, and his teeth sparkled like the finest steel.

That same day, he went to work at Number Seven furnace in one of the main mills. He worked through the evening and night and morning, and through the rest of the day. Then he went to Mrs. Horkey's boardinghouse and ate five big meals all at once. The minute he was through, he hurried back to the steel plant.

From then on, he stood in front of the huge, bubbling furnace, shoveling limestone, ore, and scrap iron into the flames. The flames licked out around him, slashing the air like red knives, but Joe Magarac only laughed as if the heat tickled him.

Pete Pussick worked at the same plant. He had been the best worker there before Joe Magarac came along. Now he had to take second place, but he said, "I have Mary Mestrovich for my wife. That satisfies me. Anyhow, that Joe is made of steel."

But even Pete was surprised when he saw Joe Magarac stirring the hot steel with his hands.

"Look at that man!" Pete shouted.

For there Joe Magarac sat in the furnace door, with the flames slapping his chin and cheeks.

"Ho! Ho!" said Joe, licking his lips. "That fire makes me glow and feel good. I'll stir that steel up some more." He put his hand down into the molten broth and stirred.

When the steel was completely cooked, and the furnace was ready to be tapped, Joe Magarac crawled out. He pushed the big bucket-like ladle out of the way and held his hands under the tap hole. The steel came hissing out, splashing into his palms.

Joe dumped the hot steel into the ingot molds which would hold and shape the steel as it cooled.

It made Pete sweat just to watch Joe Magarac. In spite of all he had seen, Pete's mouth gaped open when he saw Joe race to the lower end of the mill and grab the fresh steel in his hands. Joe squeezed the bright steel out through his fingers. He squeezed the metal like dough, and it squirted out through the fingers of each hand in straight, glistening rails. Joe made eight rails at a time.

Pete shook his head. "He'll work us all out of jobs," he said. "Joe makes more steel than all the furnaces in America put together."

Joe Magarac kept working day and night, night and day. The only time he didn't work was when he was eating. He ate everything Mrs. Horkey set before him—towers of sour-cream pan-

cakes covered with seas of syrup, garlic sausages rolled up in pastry covered with poppy seed, haunches of lamb crackling with fat, great steaming bowls of goulash with beef or veal floating in them like islands, sweetmeats and pies, and wonderful Hungarian candies.

"This gives me the strength to keep the steel cooking," Joe said. "I make so many rails now, the yard is full of them."

It was true. There were so many rails in the mill yard squeezed out by Joe Magarac's fingers that there was scarcely room for any more.

One Thursday, the mill boss walked up to Joe. "We have more rails here than we have buyers for, Magarac," the boss told him. "We'll have to shut down the mill for a few days. Put a slow heat in the furnace, so it will keep warm 'til we go back to work again."

When Pete and Eli and the others heard the plant was going to shut down for three days, they grumbled.

"When we don't work we don't get paid," Pete said.

Eli said, "It's that Joe Jackass's fault."

"Joe Magarac is a good man," Pete said, "but he works too much."

Joe walked past then, cinder streaks on his face, his head down. He looked sad and thoughtful.

"Hey, Magarac," said Eli, "how are we men going to feed our families if we lose work? You better stop making so much steel."

Joe Magarac said, "Ho, ho!" but there was no laughter in his voice. "America needs plenty of steel. What we need is a bigger mill here, the biggest in the whole Monongahela Valley. We'll build the new mill out of the best steel anywhere."

Eli said, "This mill is good enough for me. I just don't want it to shut down."

Pete and Eli went home. As Pete walked toward his house he felt happy, in spite of being out of work until Monday. Mary had planted geraniums and petunias all around the little lawn in front of their place, and the color of the flowers gave a sparkle to the smoky air.

When he walked in the door, Pete told Mary, "The mill's closing down for three days. We'll all get a good rest."

Mary looked off toward Mrs. Horkey's boardinghouse. "Poor Joe Magarac," she said. "What will he do if he can't work every minute?"

110

On Monday, Pete and the rest of the steelworkers went back to the mill. Pete looked toward Number Seven furnace, expecting to see Joe shoveling scrap and limestone through the door. There was no sign of Joe. Another man was working in his place.

Pete looked toward the end of the huge building, expecting to see Joe squeezing out steel rails through his fingers. Joe was not there either.

"Where's Joe Magarac?" Pete asked the melter boss.

"Maybe he's taking a rest," the melter boss said, laughing. A voice nearby said, "How's the steel look this time?"

"Who's that?" the boss asked, looking all around.

"Ho! Ho!" the voice boomed. "It's me, Joe Magarac. I'm inside this bucket ladle."

Pete stared, and the boss started toward the pouring platform. There, sitting in the big ladle which was filled with boiling steel, was Joe. The steel was bubbling up around his neck.

"You crawl up out of there, Joe!" the boss yelled. "You're going to melt down, otherwise."

Joe Magarac showed his teeth in a grin. "That's what I want. I'm sick of a mill that won't work for three whole days. I'm made of the best steel anywhere. You wait while I melt down, and then pour me into the mold. Next, take that steel with me mixed in it and roll it out into beams and girders to build the new mill. That new mill will make more jobs and turn out the best steel in America."

Pete Pussick shook his head. "You sure that's what you want to do, Joe?" he asked.

"That will make me happy," Joe said. "You tell your Mary she's as pretty as steel shining in the sunrise."

Before Pete could open his mouth, Joe Magarac ducked down and disappeared. The melter boss did as Joe had told him to do.

When the men poured the steel and rolled it out, the steel was so bright and perfect, it shone like a silver mirror.

"That's the most perfect steel there ever was," Pete said.

And the boss said, "We're going to build the new mill with it. Joe Magarac made that steel, and he's shining inside it. We're going to build the finest mill any man has seen."

"He was the greatest steelman that ever lived," Pete said. He turned away, thinking that he heard Joe Magarac laughing up through the girders and sparks and smoke. There was a shovel lying nearby where a worker had dropped it. Pete wasn't looking, and he stumbled and went sprawling.

The men laughed as he picked himself up.

Eli Stanoski called out, "Hey, *magarac,* I guess you should pick up your feet."

Pete started to turn his hands into fists. No one was going to call him a jackass and get away with it. Then he remembered Joe Magarac, the greatest steelman of all. He felt proud to be called by Joe's name.

Pete let his hands fall to his sides, and he laughed. "Let's get to work building the new mill," he said.

They did, and the mill stands to this day, its furnaces burning against the night sky like a tall sunset. Other new, bright mills stand beside it. And the strong men working among the furnaces and the ingot molds and the presses still tell the story of Joe Magarac.

If someone yells at them, "Hey, *magarac!*" they laugh, "Ho! Ho!" and flex their muscles with pride and work even harder.